THE
ETERNAL
CITY

By Mike Dunbar

Illlustrations by

Sara Haley Santaniello

All characters and events in this book are fictional.

Any resemblance to persons living or dead is coincidental.

Copyright © 2013 Soul Star Publishing, LLC and Mike Dunbar

Published through Createspace by Soul Star Publishing,

ISBN-13: 978-1497311077

ISBN-10: 1497311071
© 2014 Mike Dunbar

DEDICATION

To all my wonderful and supporting fans who believed
enough to make the Castleton Series a reality.

CONTENTS

ACKNOWLEDGMENTS

A special thank you to Sara Haley Santaniello for her wonderful illustrations, and her ability to capture exactly what the author was looking for. Thank you to Heidi Angell for editing, layout, and believing in the series enough to publish the series, despite the author's platform being "the wrong market". In advance, thank you to Richard Newman, a fantastic artist who is going to be redoing the covers for the whole series. Look forward to the Second editions coming out over the next several months.

CHAPTER ONE
THE TRIUMVIRATE

"Alayniess! Oh, Alayniess! Eternal city. You are so old no one knows when you came to be or who built you. You have always been and we thought you would last forever. Now, I am all alone to witness your end and what I see has broken my heart." Carolus Nukium sat on the top step of a wide, stone staircase that led up to a large stone building.

Carolus was middle aged. His wavy hair was dark brown, with streaks of gray on his temples and around his ears. His bushy mustache had streaks of gray in it as well. He was a short man, around five feet tall. Seeing his face, you would know right away that he was usually a happy man. The pattern of lines at the corners of his eyes and mouth indicated that he spent most of his time wearing a broad smile. Not today. He held his face in his hands and was crying.

The building behind Carolus was in the center of a magnificent city. The staircase he sat on rose so high he could see his city stretched out below him. As high as he was, he could not see the city's end. It was that big. The most beautiful and famous cities in history – Athens and Rome – would not be built for another 10,000 years, but if their builders could have visited Alayniess, they would have burned with jealousy. The Greeks and Romans worked in white marble, a soft stone that is easy to cut and carve. Marble will last for many thousands of years. Alayniess was built of polished granite, one of the hardest of all stones. Granite will last forever. An eternal city has to be built of granite.

Granite is found all over the world. Large blocks of it are cut from mountain sides to be made into building materials. The site where granite is cut is called a quarry. Each quarry produces its own colors and patterns. People who work with this stone can look at a piece of granite and tell what country it came from, sometimes even the specific quarry. The people who built Alayniess used these different colors and textures to create buildings so beautiful they could only be believed by seeing them. To obtain different patterns Alaynians had searched the world. They brought back massive slabs of different colors and patterns of granite to their continent to create their city.

The building standing behind and above Carolus was obviously an important one. Anyone looking at it knew it was either the government center or a temple, as it was topped by a large ornate dome made of yellow granite. The stone was as smooth as glass and reflected the tropical sun. It was so brilliant the building looked like a star come down to earth.

Although Carolus was crying, he had not come to this place to weep. He had come to beg, to beg one last time for his city. Once again, he had been turned away and his emotions had overcome him. He sat on a granite step and his grief poured out of him. He raised his head from his hands and with red, swollen eyes stared at the activity in the open plaza below him. There, a group of Alaynians were moving a massive granite block as big as two school busses. They went about their work as if nothing were wrong.

The Alaynians did not pull the huge stone blocks with ropes, like in the pictures of Egyptian workers building the pyramids. Instead, four Alaynians, one standing at each corner, guided the block with a stick-like tool. The granite block floated above the ground at about waist level, and glided slowly forward. When its path needed to be corrected, the four Alaynians moved their wand-like tools and the block responded.

The granite block was bright green. It was not shaped like a big brick, with straight sides and square corners. Instead, it resembled a piece to a gigantic, three-dimensional jig saw puzzle. When the four Alaynians reached the wall where it was to be fitted, they raised their wands. This elevated the massive granite piece upward until it was slightly higher than an opening of the same shape. Then, the four workers used their wands to move the block precisely over the opening. Finally, they slowly lowered it into place. The block fit into the wall so perfectly the joints between the new piece and those already in place disappeared. The texture and color of the granite block matched perfectly the color and texture of the wall. The building under construction looked like it was a single surface of unbroken granite.

Carolus turned his head to watch the work going on at a second construction site near the first. In this site, three statues were being carved in gray granite. The statues were as high as church steeples and stood in a row overlooking the plaza below. Even though they were incomplete, enough work had been done so Carolus knew who the statues honored. The two end statues were women, while the one in the middle was a man. All three looked so much alike there could be no doubt; the people they represented were closely related. Perhaps even sisters and a brother.

The carvers held rods like the ones being used by the workers moving the large building block, only these rods were shorter. The carvers used their rods to carefully slice away granite from the statues. For them, carving granite was like an ice sculptor using an electric chain saw to carve a block of ice. The rods sliced through the hard, dense stone as easily as a hot knife cuts through butter. The rods left behind a smooth, polished surface that needed no additional work.

"Alayniess, Alayniess," Carolus lamented. "Your art and your science almost equal those of the Gods. Look what we have created. Look at what we can do. We have harnessed nature, and nature herself has become our servant. She does as we command. We tell stones to move and they obey. How could a civilization as beautiful and advanced as ours come to this bitter end?" He burst into tears again. He placed his face in his hands and tears trickled between his fingers.

"Eternal city, your republic is as old as you," he said as he wept, his body shaking with the violence of his sobs. "We governed ourselves and every Alaynian was free. We protected our liberty and would let no one take our freedoms from us. There is no one on this earth who could destroy us from without. Who would have ever dreamed that the end would come from within? Oh Alayniess, your own children have betrayed you!"

He lifted his red, tear-stained face and looked over his shoulder at the domed building behind him. He paused a long minute before standing and climbing the last two steps. This placed him on a wide granite platform in front of the yellow-colored building.

Carolus walked to the building until he reached a line of Alaynian men standing shoulder-to-shoulder, the length of the platform. They were all the same size as Carolus, about five feet tall. He put his face right up to another man's, so he was staring his fellow directly in the eye. Normally, two people would find it uncomfortable to be this close to one another. However, the man did not respond. He stared straight ahead. He only reacted when Carolus tried to slip between him and the man next to him. Then, the two men linked arms and shifted their legs so they crossed, one man's leg overlapping the other. At the same moment the entire line did the same thing, so like soldiers snapping to parade rest the long line became a human chain link fence. By joining their arms and crossing their legs, they closed any opening between them. As a result, Carolus could not pass anywhere along the platform. He was barred from the building by a living barrier of connected bodies.

Carolus moved down the line looking one man after another directly in the eye. None of them looked back. They all continued to stare straight ahead. Carolus came to a man he recognized. "Meekaylus," he said to his old friend. "Meekaylus, it is I, Carolus. Don't you recognize me? Our fathers were best friends. We grew up together. We have known each other all our lives. You married my sister. Speak to me, Meekaylus. You can break this trance. You are not a slave. You and I are free Alaynians." Meekaylus did not respond.

While Carolus was speaking to his mute brother-in-law, a flurry of activity and movement occurred behind the line of men. Three people had come out of the domed building and were separated from Carolus only by the row of bodies. The new arrivals were two women and a man. The three looked so much alike there was no doubt they were brother and sisters. They were all the same age, and so could be nothing other than triplets. The women were so beautiful that a man seeing them for the first time would gasp. As for the man, he was so handsome all women would welcome

8

his attention. Carolus did not react to their appearance. He knew the three, and was not affected by their beauty.

"Carolus Nukium," said one of the women, her voice dripping with sarcasm. "You are so tiresome. I don't have to ask why you have come back. It's for the same reason you have visited us before: time, after time, after time. You want the Triumvirate to stop its progress and give back your precious republic. It is not going to happen. Alayniess belongs to us now, as do the Alaynians. We are building an empire that will be far more glorious than the old republic. We are not going to stop because of your endless begging. So, stop. You sound like an annoying sea bird– pleeez, pleeez."

Carolus threw himself against the line of men. Their linked arms and crossed legs acted like a trampoline. He merely bounced off them. The men did not even blink. They just stared ahead. "Ha," the man with the two women laughed at Carolus' futile efforts. "Carolus, take my advice. The time has come for you to leave Alayniess. You don't belong here anymore. We don't know why you are not in a trance. Why out of all the people in Alayniess, are you alone immune? However, even if you are unaffected, you can't stop us. Since you find our empire so distasteful, why don't you go to the snowy lands to the east? Join those other types of men that live in caves and wear animal skins? They attach sharp stones to the ends of sticks to hunt meat. Maybe they will take you in and teach you how to sharpen a stone. Then, you can come back with weapons and try to stop the Triumvirate. Or, you could stay with them and build a republic for them. I'm sure a republic would appeal to people so primitive. They don't have the intelligence to understand the glories of an empire. You'll fit right in."

"Congrata, Exeta, Lexitus," Carolus said, holding his hands together as if praying. "I knew you as children. Please listen to me. Alayniess educated you, nurtured you, and raised you. You have always held such promise. Even when you were young, it was obvious you had been blessed with great ability. You could have been honored and respected servants of your city and your people. I don't know what causes this trance. I only know you are using it to control Alaynians. I don't know why I don't go into the trance so that you can control me. I don't know why you three don't go into the trance. I don't why those who live in the country don't go into the trance, unless they come into Alayniess. But I beg you, stop what you are planning. Work with me to free our fellow Alaynians from the trance and to return their freedom to them."

"We are doing something even greater," the woman Exeta replied. "Although you do not think so, the Triumvirate does serve Alayniess. We are making Alayniess even greater than she was under the republic."

"Your Triumvirate serves the Triumvirate. You are glorifying yourselves," Carolus argued. "Alayniess never built statues to honor those who serve the city. Now, you are erecting statues to yourselves, statues taller than most buildings. This is ego. This is pride. This is not the service Alaynians have always given freely and without payment. This is control, not the freedom Alaynians have always enjoyed."

"I will tell you one final time, Carolus," the man Lexitus said, anger replacing his earlier mocking tone. "Leave Alayniess! You don't belong here anymore. Go make your life elsewhere, perhaps with the primitives. If you stay here you will go on being miserable for the rest of your life. However, you will never be able to stop the Triumvirate. We are too powerful. Go!"

The two women and the man turned and reentered the building. Carolus returned to his step, sat down, and began to cry again. Again, he sobbed so forcefully that his whole body shook.

CHAPTER TWO
CHAZ

Chaz Newcomb entered his father's office with a big smile on his face. "Hello, Mr. Takahashi," he said, greeting his father's secretary. Mr. Takahashi looked up and couldn't help but smile back at Chaz's joyful expression. The young man's happiness was electric and catching. Chaz was an archaeologist at the University of New Hampshire. The Time Institute, where his father worked was part of UNH, so the father and son saw each other nearly every day. As a result, Mr. Takahashi knew the young man well.

"Is my Dad in?" Chaz asked, pointing at his father's office. Mr. Takahashi nodded and waved his hand to tell Chaz to enter. Chaz was the young man's nickname. His real name was Charles, just like his father, just like his grandfather, just like his great-grandfather. Just like every one of his ancestors as far back as the family could remember.

Dr. Charles Newcomb was sitting at his desk correcting exams. He greeted his son with enthusiasm. "Chaz," he said, standing and opening his arms to hug his son. "This is a wonderful surprise," he added as the two embraced. Chaz looked very much like a younger version of his father. The only major difference was that Dr. Newcomb had a bushy mustache that had gone white, while Chaz was clean shaven. However, both had the same wavy hair. His father's hair was well on its way to turning gray, while Chaz's was still dark brown. Chaz had also inherited his father's perpetual smile and twinkling blue eyes. Those eyes were intelligent, with humor and compassion mixed in. Both the father and son were people anyone would like on first meeting.

There was one big difference between the two - their size. Except for their ages, a stranger seeing them at a distance would think Chaz was the father and Dr. Newcomb was his young son. While they hugged, Dr. Newcomb raised himself on his tiptoes to kiss his son's cheek. Dr. Newcomb was a teacher at the Time Institute and the Dean of Students. Like all time travelers, he was short and slight, only a little over five feet tall. Dr. Newcomb had inherited his size from his father, who had been a small man and a Fixer team pilot. His grandfather had also been small and had also been a time traveler. Chaz got his height from his mother's side, where the men were full-sized.

"Great news, Dad," Chaz bubbled as he sat down in the chair next to his father's desk. Dr. Newcomb sat down too and smiled broadly. He raised his eyebrows in an unspoken invitation for his son to tell him what had happened. "You know these seismic disturbances in the mid-Atlantic between Africa and Brazil? They've been going on for a number of years." Dr. Newcomb nodded. Yes, he had learned about these minor earthquakes on the news. Geologists were not concerned about them. Even though they occurred regularly, they were small and caused no damage. Like everyone else, Dr. Newcomb assumed they were related to shifting plates in the earth's crust. He remembered reading somewhere that in the earth's early history these plate movements had been responsible for moving the continents and pushing up mountain ranges. However, all that happened many millions of years ago, so people living today had nothing to worry about.

"I never paid much attention to these quakes either," Chaz went on. "However, I have a good friend who is a geologist at the University. These quakes are right up his alley and he has been studying them. This is the exciting part! The quakes are not caused by two of the earth's plates squeezing against each other. Something else is going on and he does not know what it is. To top it off, earlier this year a new island appeared in the middle of the Atlantic Ocean, right along the earth's equator. The island has been growing steadily as if it is being pushed up out of the sea.

"As part of his research, my friend flies over the island regularly. He takes measurements, keeping track of its growth. On his last flight he saw something incredible. There are ruins on the island. There's a city there that is so big it could take years before all of it rises above water. Dad, this is an unknown civilization and it's incredibly old. It has been kept secret from the public while the Geology Department decided what to do."

Chaz paused for dramatic effect and to let the excitement build. Then he blurted, "Dad, the University has appointed me the head archaeologist. I'm going to be leading the dig and writing the reports. This find is going to be my project. It's the most exciting thing since Heinrich Schliemann discovered the city of Troy, and I'm going to be in charge of the dig!"

Dr. Newcomb got up from his chair a second time and Chaz rose to meet him. The pair hugged tightly as Dr. Newcomb repeated. "This is so exciting, son! This is so exciting!" Finally, he released his son, went to the door and said, "Mr. Takahashi, can you call Mrs. Newcomb? She needs to hear this news too."

Three transports set down on a barren island. The transports were not airplanes. They looked very much like time craft from the Time Institute. Time craft are similar in size and shape to a Volkswagen bus, the kind of van the hippies used to drive, the kind that were covered with flowers and peace signs. However, no one would confuse a transport with a time craft. While they had the same shape, transports were as big as railroad cars. They had to be. These three craft would be the living quarters and the laboratories for a team of archaeologists, geologists, and videographers sent here by the University of New Hampshire.

The team of 12 archaeologists was led by Chaz Newcomb. The four geologists were supervised by his friend Will Nelson. The university wanted a record of the expedition's findings, and so a holovideo was being made by the three videographers.

The 19 people, plus the three transport pilots stepped out of the craft and onto the island. The place looked like an arctic desert. The entire island was bare dirt with some small stones mixed in. No plants were growing anywhere. There was no other life, no animals and no birds. The only thing that was not arctic-like was the temperature. It was 95 degrees and humid. This was not a surprise for the people on the transports. They knew that no matter how barren and polar the landscape appeared, they were on the equator, where it is always hot.

"We can leave the transports right where they are," Chaz told Will. "This location should make a good base camp. Why don't we have the crews unpack while you and I do some scouting? I need to figure out where to begin the dig, and I know you want to set up some equipment." After instructing the crews what to do,

Chaz, Will, and the head videographer set out to examine the island.

"You can see the tops of some of the buildings in the distance," Will told Chaz. "They are even more obvious when you are looking down on them from the air. I noticed that large, broken dome first. It seems to have a wide plaza in front of it. It stands above everything else, so I'm guessing it was an important place."

"Yes," Chaz agreed. "Generally, ancient civilizations built important buildings so they were taller than those around them. Government buildings and temples were often built on a hill."

"Like Capitol Hill in Washington?" Will guessed.

"Right. Capitol Hill is a good example," Chaz agreed. "I would like to inspect that dome up close. One of the first questions we asked back at UNH was who built this city, what civilization was it? I'm more likely to find that information in an important building than in a house or a shop. I assume any culture that could build a city this big had a written language. I'm hoping we'll find writing on the building. If I'm lucky it will be a known language. If not, I'm hoping to find a Rosetta Stone."

"A what?" Will asked.

"A Rosetta Stone," Chaz explained. "For centuries archaeologists were unable to read ancient Egyptian hieroglyphics, a form of picture writing. Then, in 1799 a soldier with Napoleon's army discovered a stone with ancient writing chiseled on it. The writing was the same message in two languages – Ancient Greek and Egyptian hieroglyphics. Archeologists could read Greek, and so they knew what the hieroglyphics said. The Rosetta Stone became the key that unlocked an unknown language. If we don't know this civilization's language, maybe I can find something that is also written in a language we do know."

"Where did all the dirt come from?" the videographer asked Will. "If this city was underwater, how come it's buried under all this dirt?"

"It's sediment," Will explained. "The wind carries dust from the land, from South America and Africa. The dust settles out of the air onto the ocean's surface and slowly falls down to the bottom. Small marine animals like plankton die and fall to the bottom. Over the centuries, all that dust and debris built up until it eventually buried the city."

"That will make for an easy dig," Chaz said. "Usually, archaeologists dig in places where people have lived over a long time. Each group of people leaves its own layer. So, as we pass through the layers as we dig down. Each layer has a different story to tell and we have to be careful to keep track of each story. Recording all those layers and making sense of them is called stratigraphy."

"We use stratigraphy in geology as well," Will added. "If a volcano explodes, it leaves a layer of ash. Thousands of years later, a stream flowing over the ash will leave behind a layer of sand. Then, a forest grows up and leaves another type of dirt. We study the layers to find out what geological events happened, and when."

The group reached the broken dome sticking out of the now-dry land and Chaz was able to examine the building up close. He walked all the way around the dome, taking rough measurements by counting his steps. "I know this is not an exact way to measure," he told Will and the videographer. "But I do know this dome is as big as the capitol in Washington. There must be a huge building below the ground." The stone dome was covered with a type of sea creature called barnacles. Barnacles are like small clams that grow on hard surfaces, like the bottom of a boat. Chaz pulled a knife out of his pocket and scratched away the barnacles until he reached bare stone. "It's granite," he said with surprise. "This had to be a very advanced civilization, if it worked with granite. I wonder if the whole building is granite, or just the dome. That's another question we'll be able to answer once we start digging."

"It can't be granite," said Will. "Where would they get granite out here in the middle of the Atlantic Ocean?" He examined the small patch of stone Chaz had exposed. "You're right," he agreed. "It is granite, and I can tell you exactly where it came from. This is a variety of yellow granite only found in India. That can't be. These people would have needed huge machines to cut this stuff, and huge ships to bring it here. This isn't right. This granite should not be here."

"I love a good mystery," Chaz said with a smile. "I'm going to start digging first thing tomorrow morning."

By the end of the day the archeologists and the others had completed their set up. All three teams – the archaeologists, geologists, and videographers -- would be ready to go to work first thing in the morning. As night fell they started a campfire and sat around it eating their dinner. For most of them, this was the first time they had seen a sunset at the equator. In New Hampshire, there are long sunsets and even longer periods of twilight. Nearly everyone was surprised when the sun seemed to fall into the sea and the sky quickly became dark. "That's the way the sun sets in the tropics," Will explained. "Up in New Hampshire it sets at an angle to the horizon, so sunset lasts longer. Even when the sun disappears up there, it remains close below the horizon for a long time. So, you get long twilights. Here, the sun is directly overhead. It sets in a straight line and once it is below the horizon, it just keeps on trucking. You get almost no twilight."

"Same thing in the morning," he continued. "The sun just pops up out of the dark. Because it travels directly overhead, its light is brighter than back home. You'll want to wear sunglasses and sunscreen while you're here. Here's another bit of trivia. Did you know days are all pretty much the same length at the equator? They don't get shorter in the winter and longer in the summer."

"I just noticed something else," one of the archaeologists said. "There are no bugs. I brought along insect repellant. Every other place I have dug, we get attacked by bugs."

"No bugs, yet," Will answered. "This island is so new they haven't found it. They will. Just give them time. Bugs live everywhere on earth." With that the crews went to the dormitory transport and crawled into their beds. Tomorrow promised to be a busy day.

Early the next morning Chaz led his team to the dome where he had decided to begin the dig. Before they left camp Will told the archaeologist, "I just checked my instruments. Overnight, this island rose ½ an inch. That's one inch a day, a foot in less than two weeks. This island is rising faster than anything geologists have ever seen before. It's getting bigger fast. In a year, this island will be huge!"

The archeologists laid out a grid on the ground on one side of the dome. They used strings and wooden stakes to make a checkerboard pattern. They took measurements and Chad carefully recorded the exact location of each marker. The grid was important. It allowed them to accurately record where artifacts were found. This information was important to the people at UNH who would be studying their results. Also, future archeology teams working this site would have a record of exactly where Chaz had dug.

By noon, the team began to remove dirt from a long trench. They dug carefully, but they found nothing in the dirt. The soil was just as Will had predicted. It was built up of dust and small animals that had fallen to the ocean floor. The archaeologists found small rocks that had been pushed around by ocean currents and sea shells from long-dead clams. However, there was nothing that had been made by humans.

After several days, the archeologists were standing in a trench as deep as their knees. After several weeks, the trench was so deep they used ladders to climb in and out.

Still, they had found nothing from the civilization that had built the building. All they uncovered were a few granite blocks that had broken away from the dome. Chaz was not surprised. If this civilization had sunk beneath the ocean, then no one else had ever lived here. Anything worth finding was probably down at the bottom, in the plaza.

Chaz showed Will some writing he had found on the edges of the massive granite blocks. He couldn't read it, but told Will the writing probably told workers how the blocks were supposed to fit into the building. "I'm not an expert in ancient languages," Chaz said. "But I have studied them. This alphabet is different from everything else I've seen. The writing is no help at all in identifying this civilization."

Chaz was also surprised at the complex shapes of the granite blocks he found. They were not cubes. Instead, they fitted together like a giant jig saw puzzle. "I don't know how this civilization cut granite so exactly," he said to his friend. "However, locking blocks together like this is a much stronger way of building than placing one big block on another, the way we do. This building was meant to last forever and would still be in use if this civilization hadn't been lost under the ocean. Some people used to think that aliens from outer space had helped the Egyptians build the pyramids. I wonder what they would have thought if they had seen these buildings."

A month after beginning the dig, the archaeologists' trench had reached below the dome and they were beginning to uncover the front of a beautiful building. The videographers captured all the important moments on holovideo. A couple of times each day Will and the other geologists took measurements on their instruments. Otherwise, the geologists didn't have any work to do. So, they too watched this incredible building slowly appear from the dirt.

Six weeks into the dig one of the archaeologists said she heard a strange humming. She said it was so faint; she couldn't be sure what it was. Chaz climbed down into the trench, but he could not hear the sound. A couple of days later, another woman said she heard the humming too, but only when she listened carefully. The sound was very soft. Several more days passed, and all the women on the dig could hear the humming. Some said it sounded like a small machine that was far away. Others said it sounded like a note from an instrument like a violin. They all agreed the sound was so soft it seemed to be coming from a great distance.

The next week, after digging the trench even deeper, some of the men could hear the sound. They said it was faint, while the women said it had grown louder. After another week, everyone could hear the sound. "I'm sure it's something natural," Will told Chaz. "I think the women heard the sound first because they have better hearing than men. They can detect sounds that men cannot. If we had some kids or animals, they would have heard the sound before the women. Their hearing is even more sensitive."

"What in nature could make a noise like that?" Chaz asked.

"Geologists have run into things like this before," Will answered. "When air is warmed by the sun it begins to rise. If the air passes through a small crack in a rock it acts like a whistle. This sound could be nothing more than warm air rising."

"Of course," Chaz added. "It's like the singing statue of Memnon." Will had never heard of this statue and raised his eyebrows. "There's a huge statue in Egypt that used to sing when the sun warmed the stone and air passed through it. At some point someone tried to repair the statue and the singing stopped. They actually ruined what they were trying to fix. You're right, Will," he said. "This sound is natural. There are no ghosts here."

A week later, Chaz was working at the bottom of the deep trench examining the building that was becoming more exposed each day. He noticed one of his archeologists was looking pale and weak. "Sandy," he said to her. "You don't look well. Why don't you take ten?" Sandy bent over and without speaking, picked up ten items. She put them under her arm and started up the ladder. Dumbfounded, Chaz watched her climb out of the trench. When he spoke with her later, Sandy was feeling better, but couldn't remember leaving the trench, or taking anything with her.

The next day, at the bottom of the trench Chaz called all the archaeologists together for a meeting. "We're no closer to solving the question of what civilization this is than when we first stuck a shovel in the ground," he reminded them. "In fact, we don't know anything about this people other than that they had an unknown technology. That technology allowed them to cut granite with laboratory precision. Also, we know they were amazing artists. I'm asking all of you for ideas. Think about other things we could be doing. Put your heads together."

At that, Sandy, Jean-Noel, and Kathy stood in a small circle and touched their foreheads together. "Very funny," you guys Chaz laughed. "Seriously, unless we do some innovative thinking, we'll have to dig like dogs to get to the plaza. That may be the only way we'll find answers." At that the three archeologists with their heads together fell to their knees and started to dig with the hands, throwing the dirt backward, between their legs. Chaz and the others stared in surprise. "Hey, knock it off you guys," he commanded the three. They rose up on their knees and with their hands pushed everything off a nearby table.

Chaz was stunned, but he was also afraid. It had just dawned on him, the three were not joking. Something was very wrong. "Sandy, stand up," he yelled. The woman stood, while the other kept digging like dogs. Chaz walked up to the archaeologist who stood as still as a statue. He looked her in the eye. She did not look back, but stared straight ahead. "Stand up," he told the other two. They stopped digging and stood as straight and still as Sandy. "I want you three to go back to the dormitory transport. Go to bed and stay there." The three turned and one at a time climbed the ladder out of the trench. When they were all at the top Chaz told another of his archaeologists, "Go with them and make sure they are alright. Ask Will to come down here. I want his advice."

Will climbed down into the trench to speak with his friend. Chaz told him what had happened. "I saw the three when they arrived at the transport. They look like they're hypnotized. They don't seem to be aware of anything. I spoke to them and they didn't answer."

"What could it be?" Chaz asked his friend. His eyes told the story. He was frightened. He was puzzled. And he was desperate.

"The mummy's curse," Will answered. Chaz's head snapped around to look at his friend. "Just joking," Will said. "Relax. There's some explanation. With all these small earthquakes, I suspect some gas has been released from deep in the earth. The trench is the lowest point on the island, so the gas has probably collected down here. Those three are the most sensitive to it, but it doesn't seem poisonous. Try this idea. When the three get better, have them wear respirators."

"That's a good theory," Chaz answered thoughtfully. "You know the ancient Sibyls were a group of women prophets. The Greek rulers went to them to get predictions about the future. To prophesy, the Sibyls would descend into a cave and go into a trance. Now, we know that the air in the cave had a natural gas called ethylene mixed in. They breathed the gas and went into a trance. When they went back above ground, they recovered."

"Interesting," Will said. "I know that long ago doctors used ethylene to put people to sleep before an operation. Let's give your three people a little time," he added reassuringly. "They'll be better soon enough. Then, give them masks to wear. By the way, what's going on with that humming sound? Still hearing it?"

"Yeah," Chaz responded, "off and on. It only happens in the afternoon for about an hour. As we get deeper, it's getting louder. The women members of the team swear that sometimes it sounds like music. I only hear humming."

"Curious," Will said. "I suppose if air moved through a crack in the rock fast and then slowed down, it could produce a different pitch that would sound like music. Or, if it went through a narrow crack and then into a wider one, it could sound like someone whistling a tune."

Mike Dunbar

CHAPTER THREE
THE AUCKLAND'S CREW

Dr. Newcomb was in the kitchen preparing supper when his son Chaz walked through the door. The older man was relaxing and enjoying an afternoon off from work. He had changed out of his brown teacher's uniform. He was dressed casually in shorts and a loose, short-sleeve shirt with a wild Hawaiian print on it. "Chaz," he said excitedly, dropping what he was doing to hug his son. "This is a pleasant surprise. I thought you were still on your dig."

Chaz was dressed in khaki cargo shorts, work boots, and a UNH T-shirt. He had a backpack slung over one shoulder. He was deeply tanned from his time in the tropical sun and his hair was bleached almost blond. "We've had some problems, Dad," he explained as he placed his bag on the floor. "I suspended the dig. I had to call in a med-evac transport from the university to pick up the entire expedition - my team, the geologists, and the videographers. Even the transport pilots came down with this strange condition. Right now, they're all at the UNH Medical Center being treated. The doctors are trying to figure out what this affliction is."

"Whoa, son," Dr. Newcomb said holding up his hands to indicate he did not understand the conversation. "What strange condition? You never mentioned this in any of your calls home."

"I didn't have time, Dad. It all happened so fast. Three of my team came down with it first, and then one right after another, everyone else. I'm the only one who was not affected. I was on an island with 21 people who were suddenly acting funny. I called the university and they sent a transport there right away."

"Is it a sickness?" Dr. Newcomb asked.

"No, Dad. It's a condition. It's like a hypnotic trance. People become like robots and will do whatever they are told. I had to be very careful not to use any slang expressions. If they could interpret something the wrong way, they would." Chaz told his father about what happened when he said dig like a dog and knock it off. "I'm glad I never said anything like drop dead, or take a flying leap!"

"Very interesting and curious," Dr. Newcomb said. "They took everything literally? Look, your mother will be home soon. Then, Rabbi Cohen and his wife are coming over for supper. Why don't you stay and eat with us? I'm making spaghetti. You always liked that."

Chaz agreed and went up to his room to shower and change.

The Cohens arrived at six o'clock. There was no need for introductions. The Rabbi and his wife had known Chaz since the day he was born. They had visited Mrs. Newcomb and her new son at the hospital when he was only hours old. As Chaz grew, they had attended every school play and sporting event he was involved in. They had attended Chaz's graduation from UNH. Rabbi and Mrs. Cohen hugged their friends and Chaz. "Shalom, my boy. Shalom," the rabbi said in greeting. "It is so good to have you back. I can't wait to hear about your work. Being assigned this dig is a major accomplishment, my boy. I hear the archeology department at UNH is all abuzz over it. It's a major step in your career."

At dinner, the talk soon turned to Chaz's reason for coming back early. He explained the events at the dig. He described the strange humming and told how some of the women archaeologists thought it sounded more like music. It was so soft no one could be sure. It only happened for about an hour each afternoon. He explained the hypnotic trance that had caused UNH to bring everyone back to the medical center. Chaz gave Will's explanations for both the sound and the trance, rising air passing through cracks in rock and a volcanic gas.

"Your father teaches Ethics and I teach History of Time Travel," the Rabbi said. "This is beyond us. I don't know anything about geology or music and can't offer any advice. However, I think I can recommend someone who can help you with the music question." He looked at Dr. Newcomb, who immediately knew what his friend was thinking. "I suggest we contact Miss Tymoshenko, Charles. She is an experienced music history researcher. She should be able to determine whether or not this sound is music or something natural."

Dr. Newcomb nodded in agreement. "I'll make the arrangements right away," he said, rising from the table. "I know the Auckland's crew returned from a mission two days ago. They should be staying in their quarters." Dr. Newcomb returned five minutes later and announced, "Chaz, Jacob, we have a meeting with Miss Tymoshenko and her friends tomorrow morning at 9:00 in Room 307."

Chaz sat between his father and Rabbi Cohen at a large oval conference table in Room 307. At 9:00 three small, young women in red researcher uniforms entered and enthusiastically greeted Dr. Newcomb and Rabbi Cohen. Chaz made note that the three were all very attractive. One had smooth, chocolate-colored skin. Her black hair was so shiny it almost seemed a deep blue. Another had olive-colored skin and dark brown hair that was cut almost as short as his. Her eyes were light gray. However, the one with the long, auburn hair caught his attention. Most redheads have blue eyes, but hers were brown. It was a very dramatic contrast. Her skin was creamy white, except for the blush of rose on her cheeks.

Rabbi Cohen made the introductions. "Ladies, this is Dr. Newcomb's son Chaz. Chaz, this is the Auckland's crew; Lenore Smith the engineer, Jen Canfield the pilot, and Aleksandra Tymoshenko the S/O." Chaz's heart skipped. So, the redhead was the music researcher. If she agreed to help him, he would be working with her. Chaz spent much of his time on archeological digs. In his line of work that is referred to as being "in the field." In the field, the only people he saw were the other archaeologists. So, Chaz didn't meet a lot of girls and didn't date a lot. In fact, his life was pretty lonely. Maybe that could change, he thought, thanks to this strange sound being heard at the dig.

The girls took their places around the table. Chaz told the researcher team about his assignment to head the dig on the newly formed island, and the ruins that were found there. He described the dig and what he and his team had learned. Then, he told them about the sound. Finally, he talked about the strange hypnotic trance that had overcome everyone but him.

"Rabbi Cohen suggested we contact you, Miss Tymoshenko," Dr. Newcomb said. "He thought you might have some insights into this sound, or maybe music. Whatever it is."

"It's fascinating," the redhead replied. "I don't know how I could identify the sound without hearing it. Would it be possible for me to visit the dig?"

Chaz nodded. This was wonderful, he thought to himself. He would spend time on a tropical island with this beautiful researcher. No matter that the island was a desert. It would become paradise if she were there with him.

"We haven't any missions scheduled, Allie," the woman with the short hair said. What was her name, Chaz asked himself? He was so taken with the redhead he hadn't listened to the introductions as carefully as he should have. A name popped into his head. Yes, Jen. That was it. "Lenore and I can take you there in the Auckland," Jen continued. "This sounds fascinating and I would love to get in on it." Chaz made note that Jen had called her redheaded friend Allie, rather than Aleksandra. So, that was her nickname, the name her friends knew her by. He wanted to get beyond the formal tone used at the Time Institute, to a level of friendship that would allow him to call her Allie too.

"Then, it's all set," Allie said to Chaz with a friendly smile. "The Auckland has a power amplifier, so it can carry the additional weight of a fourth person, even a full-sized person. However, you may find it a bit cramped." Lenore and Jen both laughed. They remembered Charlie Newcomb, Chaz's many greats grandfather, a World War II Navy flier. He had to sit on the floor so he could fit in the small time craft. "Do you think we could be ready to go by tomorrow morning?" Allie asked Jen and Lenore. Her two crew mates nodded.

"The island is on the equator, so it will be warm there," Chaz advised. "Bring light clothing."

Jen set the Auckland down next to the abandoned transports that had brought the archeological team to the island. Those larger craft had served as their lab and dormitory. The Auckland's crew and Chaz stepped out into the tropical heat. "Whoa," Lenore said. "I see what you meant about it being warm. This is hotter than I expected. I need to get out of this uniform." One at a time, the girls went into the craft and changed. Each came out wearing shorts and a T-shirt.

"Let me show you around," Chaz offered. "We can go down into the trench later."

Chaz was being polite. There wasn't much to see on the island. Only months before, it had been the ocean floor. But he did his best at giving the girls a tour. The group arrived at the dome sticking up out of the now-dry ground. The huge dome was a marvel and seemed so odd out here in the middle of nowhere, and in the middle of an empty island. Chaz told his guests the little he knew about this culture. It had an advanced technology, but everything else was still a mystery. They had found writing, but he hadn't been able to decipher it. He explained that the building was made of granite and that this stone was very hard and difficult to work. To top it off, this type of granite had come from India, nearly halfway around the world. He also described the complex way the blocks fit together, like pieces of a giant, three-dimensional jig saw puzzle.

Being researchers, the Auckland's crew was curious about anything new and unknown. However, they usually did music research, as that was Allie's specialty. They couldn't give Chaz any advice about this project. After admiring the broken dome and the front of the building that had been exposed by the trench, Jen told Allie, "Lenore and I have to go back to the Institute to catch up on paperwork. I've got to file flight reports from our last mission and Lenore has to submit maintenance schedules. We'll leave you two here to figure out that sound. We'll be back by the end of the week. That should give you enough time to get to the bottom of things."

Chaz was pleased when Jen and Lenore's craft disappeared. He was now alone on the island with this beautiful redhead. However, he was nervous. He wanted her to like him and didn't want to make any mistakes. "For you to hear the music, we'll have to go down into the trench and wait," he suggested. "I'll bring you a chair to sit on. Meanwhile, I should keep on digging. We can talk while I work. In case it was a volcanic gas that caused my team to go into a trance, you should wear this respirator mask. It covers your whole face, but you can talk and hear."

Allie sat in a chair at the bottom of the trench wearing the mask while Chaz loosened dirt with a trowel and scooped it into a bucket. Then, he hoisted the bucket up to ground level. He repeated that over and over. As the trench lowered he exposed more and more of the front of the granite building. "So, how did you become a researcher?" he asked awkwardly, trying to start a conversation with Allie. He didn't realize that Allie was a natural conversationalist and talking to her was as easy as breathing. She explained that when she was a student in the Ukraine a guidance counselor had suggested she study at the Institute. She was the right height and weight for time travel, although her real interest was music. Since the Institute needed music researchers, it was a good fit. She really liked the Institute. The teachers there were great. Chaz's father was her favorite. Now that she was a crew member, Dr. Newcomb was a good friend. She loved Jen and Lenore. They lived together in the same apartment at the crew quarters. They had done lots of missions together. They knew each other's families and spent a lot of time together after work.

"How did you get into archaeology?" she asked Chaz. He explained that he had always loved history and the past. When he was a boy, he wanted to be a time traveler like his father. That dream ended when he grew too tall and heavy. Since he couldn't study the past by going there, he would study it by digging it out of the ground. He admired the peoples who lived in the past. They did so many amazing things. They made so many beautiful objects and built so many magnificent buildings.

"That reminds me of something your father told us when we were cadets," Allie said. "He told us people in the past were as smart as we are. The only thing they didn't have was our technology. So, they did amazing things with the technology they did have." She paused. "Ssshhh! I hear something." Allie got down on her hands and knees and listened. She heard a humming. The sound lasted about an hour. When it stopped Allie said, "I'm not sure. The sound does change pitch, but I'm not hearing any patterns that would tell me it was music. Changes in pitch could happen naturally. Rising air can speed up and slow down."

When the sound stopped Chaz and Allie called it a day. They climbed out of the trench. They went back to the transports and Chaz made supper for them. After they had eaten he suggested a walk along the ocean. This was an island and there was beach all around it. As they walked the two continued to talk about their lives, their work, and their families. Allie had never seen a tropical sunset and was amazed at how fast it got dark. When they returned to the transports they sat outside on the ground and Chaz showed her the stars. Working in the field, he spent many nights studying the sky and he knew all the constellations. He pointed them out to Allie. The night was warm and the ocean breeze was pleasant. Chaz suggested that rather than going into the transports, they take their sleeping bags outside and sleep under the sky.

When Allie awoke the next morning Chaz had already cooked her breakfast. After they had eaten he cleaned up and suggested they go back to the trench. They spent this second day just as they had the one before. Chaz continued to dig and hoist dirt out of the trench while Allie sat in a chair wearing her mask. The two chatted easily. Late in the afternoon Allie heard the sound again. Once again she got down on her hands and knees to hear better. When the sound ended she told Chaz, "I think it may be music. The patterns I heard yesterday repeated. Not only were they the same as yesterday, they repeated like parts of a song. It would be hard to find a natural explanation for that."

Like the day before, the two returned to the beach. This time, Chaz suggested they wear bathing suits and go swimming. In the tropics the sea water is warm and crystal clear. As they walked along the shore to dry off, Chaz thought how pleasant it was being with Allie. She was so nice and so easy to talk with he didn't want Jen and Lenore to come back. He wished he and this beautiful redhead could stay on this island forever, just the two of them. He thought he should tell Allie how he felt, but he was afraid. What if she didn't feel the way he did? The rest of their stay would be embarrassing and awkward. He decided to keep his feelings to himself and to see if Allie would give him some sign that she felt the same.

The third day was a repeat of the first two. This time Allie told Chaz she was sure this was music. It sounded the same as the day before. The patterns were clearer and repeated just like a chorus. She had no idea where music could be coming from, but she was sure this was music, not rising air or something natural. There was another odd thing. The music sounded more

41

like voices than instruments. She couldn't explain that either. "You did say these people had an advanced technology. Perhaps they built something that creates music, something that sings automatically. Can you imagine living back then and visiting this plaza? It would have been fascinating to hear a machine or a device that sang. It would have been a real wonder. Let's come back tomorrow and listen again. That will be my last chance before Jen and Lenore return. Maybe I can make out more detail."

Chaz nodded unhappily. Allie had just mentioned that Jen and Lenore were due back tomorrow. Soon, their time alone on the island would be over. They would all return to the Time Institute. Maybe he would see her again, but they would never be this alone. Back home, there would always be other people around. He realized he needed to work up his courage soon and tell Allie how he felt, or he may never get another chance. "Let's stop work for today," he suggested as he arranged his tools for his next work day. He didn't know when that would be. He wouldn't find out until he got back to the medical center to check up on his team. "You climb out first, Allie," he said to his companion. He couldn't see her face clearly though her respirator mask, but he watched as she started up the ladder and admired her silky auburn hair.

Chaz climbed out of the trench and found Allie gazing at the sea, still wearing her respirator. He sensed this was the time. He had to act. He stood in front of her and took off her mask. She didn't resist or try to stop him. Holding the mask in his hand he said, "I love you, Allie. Kiss me." It happened just as he dreamed. Allie raised her face to his with her lips pursed. He closed his eyes and kissed her. He dropped the respirator and put his arms around the small researcher, pulling her to him. They kissed and kissed and kissed. "Oh, Allie," he whispered in her ear. "Hold me tight. Never let me go."

Allie wrapped her arms around Chaz in a tight grip. He noted that she was stronger than he imagined, or maybe she was feeling the same emotions he was. Yes. That was it. She was gripping him with such force because she loved him as he loved her. Chaz kissed Allie's cheek, her forehead, and her ear while she continued to hold him. After a while her grip became uncomfortable and felt strange. It never let up. He took Allie's two cheeks in his hands and bent her face upward so he could look into his lover's eyes. He would tell her how happy he was that she loved him too. As soon as he saw her eyes, he pulled back. "Oh, no!" he exclaimed in a loud cry. "Oh no, Allie. Not you too!"

Allie stared straight ahead with a vacant look. She was not aware of Chaz or where she was. Tears filled Chaz's eyes. The love the two had just expressed was not real. In a hypnotic trance Allie was just doing whatever he said. She had kissed him because he had told her to. She had held him tightly and never let go because he had said that too. As he led Allie back to the transports he was overwhelmed with sadness. He had lost his new love. More exactly, he never really had it. It was an illusion. Furthermore, he had brought a woman he loved to a place that had caused her harm. He was overwhelmed with guilt, and at the same time overwhelmed with loss.

When the Auckland arrived the next day, Chaz ran up to Jen and Lenore. The look of horror on his face told the two time travelers something was very wrong. They looked around the camp and spotted Allie sitting in a chair. She seemed safe and well. After all, what could be wrong on an island in the middle of the ocean? "What is it, Chaz?" Lenore asked. "What's wrong?"

"It's Allie. She has gone into the same trance as everyone else."

"Didn't you make her wear a respirator?" Jen asked accusingly, breaking into a run toward Allie.

"Yes. Yes, I did," Chaz called as he tried to catch up with Jen.

Jen and Lenore fell to their knees in front of Allie, who stared straight ahead. "Allie, Allie," Lenore said firmly while patting her cheek. "Allie, can you hear me?"

Jen, Lenore, and Chaz walked into Allie's room at the UNH medical center. She was in bed, and stared straight up at the ceiling. Her doctor came in and spoke with them. "This appears to be the same condition that overcame the others on your team, Mr. Newcomb. We don't know what causes the trance, but the good news is that it wears off without any aftereffects. I predict

Miss Tymoshenko will be fine in a day or two. We'll do a few tests, but unless we find something different about her case, we will release her when she becomes aware."

"Doctor," Jen said to the physician, "We have a mystery on our hands that is more than just medical. However, in order to put this puzzle together we need to know everything you know. I've contacted Dr. Newcomb and Rabbi Cohen at the Time Institute. Can you join us in Room 307 at the MacDonald Center Monday morning at 9:00? Allie should be well by then and she can tell us what she learned about the sound. Chaz, you should be there too, and please bring your friend Will, the geologist. We need his knowledge as well."

Sitting around the conference table Allie looked and acted normal. She had recovered completely and was her same old happy, friendly self. Chaz looked at her and his heart squeezed. She remembered nothing that he had said to her. She had forgotten their kisses and their hugs.

"It seems we have three mysteries here," Jen said, starting the meeting. "First, we have a city no one can identify. Second, we have a strange condition that takes over everyone there – everyone but you, Chaz. And third, we have an unidentified sound that may be music."

"There is not much I can tell you about the city that I haven't already told you," Chaz added. "The building we are excavating is made of granite that comes from India. Someone brought it half way around the world to a place that was once in the middle of the Atlantic Ocean between Africa and South America, right on the equator. The granite blocks were cut and fitted together in a complex manner. The builders must have used some unknown technology. The people had writing, but no one can read it. We have no idea who they were. Until we find something we can date, we don't even know when this city was occupied, or when it sank into the sea."

"I'm a scientist," Will said, speaking next. "I still believe there is a scientific explanation for what has happened. I've explained to Chaz how rising air passing through cracks in rock could make sounds. I told him how volcanic gases could put people into what appears to be a trance. However, I've checked my instruments and they never detected any gas. As far as I can tell there was nothing there but the sea air. So, I cannot prove my theory."

"I don't believe the sound is caused by rising air," Allie said. "It has complex patterns that repeat every day and during every event. I don't think nature can create melody. I believe it's a song. Before I went into my trance, I thought it was voices, not instruments. It was just too faint to be sure."

Jen turned to the doctor. "What did you find out?" she asked.

"The trance turns off the part of the brain that we're using right now, the part that is our consciousness," the doctor explained. "This means the person is in a dream-like state. It's a condition that medicine calls somnambulism. The word literally means sleepwalking. The difference is that we can wake up a sleepwalker. The people in this trance need a couple of days to wake up. They wake up slowly, but then, they are just as normal as any other sleepwalker. Just like a sleepwalker, they don't remember much of the experience. They may have some dim memories, like we all have about our dreams, but that is all." Chaz glanced at Allie for any hint she remembered their kisses. She did not react; she was listening to the doctor. "We have no idea what causes the trance. Our tests found no traces of any gas in the team's blood samples. We have no more answers than the rest of you."

"That explains why the respirator didn't work for me," Allie said. "The trance wasn't caused by gas. What else could it be? There's another question. Chaz, why are you the only one who isn't affected? What is different about you? Doctor, do you have any theories?"

"Since we don't know what causes the trance, it could be anything," the doctor said, shrugging his shoulders. "It could be genetic. If the trance is caused by a germ, he could be immune. There could be a dozen reasons. We won't know why Chaz is unaffected until we find out what's causing the trance."

"The discovery of this unknown city is too important. We can't walk away from it," Rabbi Cohen added. "We're part of a university. Learning is what we do. However, we can't ask archeologists and geologists to go back to the dig. We've been lucky so far. No one has been hurt."

"Yes," Chaz agreed. "This discovery is one of the most important in the history of archaeology. We can't abandon it."

The table fell silent while everyone pondered the problem. "There is only one solution," Jen said thoughtfully. "We need to go back in time and find the answers there."

"How will you find the time when the city was occupied?" Dr. Newcomb asked. "You don't know the sequences. They're not in the directory because they have never been mapped. Until now, we didn't know this city ever existed."

"I'm not sure how we'll do it," Jen answered. "However, if anyone can figure out a way to find the sequences, it's the CT 9225's crew. My plan is to go back to the time before that city disappeared into the sea. I worry there could be danger. If there is, I want Patrick Weaver and his team as my back up."

Dr. Newcomb and Rabbi Cohen both nodded in agreement. "You're right, Miss Canfield," the rabbi announced. "Would you and your team be willing to visit the CT 9225's crew and ask them to join us here? We'll send both of you on the mission together."

CHAPTER FOUR
DR. MACDONALD

Sixteen year-old Patrick Weaver stepped away from the cash register in the Atlantic Academy lunch hall. He had a meal on his tray and he carried his back pack slung over his right shoulder. Patrick was now a sophomore in high school. He had not grown much in the past year. He was still short and muscular. He still had freckles on his nose, but the ones on his face had disappeared. His voice had grown deeper and he had sandy-colored fuzz on his face that was soon going to turn into a beard. Meanwhile, Patrick didn't have to shave.

Patrick looked around the hall until he spotted his friend Mike Castleton sitting at a table by himself. Mike had his nose in a book and was unaware of anything around him. He didn't even look up as Patrick slid into the chair across the table.

Mike had grown an inch in this last year. He knew that, because every birthday his father measured his height by marking it on a board attached to the wall. Mike had a record of how much he had grown each year going back to age two, when he could first stand. Mike's face had lengthened and was no longer round like a soccer ball. His ears didn't stand out from his head any more. His thick, dark-brown hair would curl if he didn't keep it short. He still had beautiful, blue eyes with long, thick lashes and thick eyebrows. The freckles that covered his face were still there, but weren't as noticeable as when he was younger. Mike had begun to shave. If he did not run a razor over his face every day, he would quickly grow a full-face beard. In the past year, Mike Castleton had become a young man.

"Whadda, ya reading," Patrick asked.

"Anthropology text book," Mike answered, holding up the book's cover for his friend to see.

"Let me give you a tip," Patrick said in a stage whisper to let Mike know he was joking. "In high school, when kids take electives, they choose easy classes, like art or band. They already have enough work to do, so they don't add to their burden by taking tough subjects like anthropology. What does that word mean anyway?"

"Anthropology?" Mike said. "It's the study of human beings. It's only the most important subject of all. And being an S/O on a time team, it's stuff I have to know."

"Like what?" Patrick asked, still teasing his friend.

"Did you know human beings began in Africa millions and millions of years ago?" Mike asked. "Did you know there have been lots of different types of humans? There were actually many different species. A lion is a different species from a tiger; even though they are both cats. So, one species of humans looked different from another. Some species were taller, and others were short. Some were smart and used tools, while some ate plants and whatever else they could find. This is real important to know, because today there is only one species – us. We're called homo sapiens. That's Latin for thinking man. However, anthropologists call us modern humans."

Mike grew enthusiastic as he elaborated on this story. "Humans started in Africa and we stayed there for most of the time we have been on earth. Humans didn't move into the rest of the world until recently. Well, it was hundreds of thousands of years ago, but that's a short time compared to the millions we've been around. When humans left Africa they went north through what today are Egypt, Israel, and Lebanon. Then, they came to a fork in the road, except there weren't really any roads. I was just using that as expression so you'd understand humans were on the move." Patrick rolled his eyes. "Some humans went east into Asia, others went west into Europe. The people that chose Europe ran into a problem. The area was in an Ice Age. So, they stayed in the south, in places like France, Italy, and Spain. It was still pretty darned cold there, but at least those areas weren't buried under a glacier."

"Yawn," Patrick said mockingly, opening his mouth wide and patting it with his hand.

"Those first people in Europe were called Neanderthals," Mike continued, too excited to notice his friend was making fun of him. "The Neanderthals lived in Europe for thousands and thousands of years all by themselves. They usually made their homes in caves, so we call them cavemen. Then, a new species came up out of Africa. It was us, our ancestors, modern humans. The modern humans moved into the same places as the Neanderthals and the two species lived near each other for thousands of more years. They didn't have any choice but to live in the same places. The rest of Europe was under this huge glacier.

"A lot of the earth's water was frozen into thick ice sheets that covered the northern part of the world. Because so much water was frozen, the oceans were a lot lower. That means there was more dry land. Today, a lot of the places that were land back then are under the sea. Once upon a time, people could walk on dry ground from France to England and to Ireland. They weren't islands back then. That's how the Native Americans got here. They walked over a land bridge between Russia and Alaska."

Patrick put his head on his arms, pretending to sleep. He even snored. As he did, their other friend Nick

Pope came to the table carrying his lunch tray. Nick was still tall and thin. This year he had broken six feet, but had not gained a pound. His wild, dark hair still refused to stay combed. Nick too had to shave, but his beard was not as heavy as Mike's. Nick's expression was the same as when he was younger. He always looked serious, like he was worried. He still didn't make jokes and usually didn't get them when someone else was being funny.

Nick pointed his thumb at Patrick with a quizzical look on his face, a gesture that asked Mike, "What's with him?" Mike shook his head to indicate Patrick was not really sleeping, but was only being silly.

"We're talking about early humans," Mike explained to Nick. "Our direct ancestors and the Neanderthals were neighbors, but they didn't look alike. Neanderthals were short and very strong. They probably had red or sandy-colored hair. Modern humans looked just like us. We're no different now than we were back then."

"That explains Patrick," Nick said without any expression. "He's short and strong with sandy hair. You must be a Neanderthal, Patrick." Patrick still pretended to sleep and snore.

"Hey Nick," Mike said with surprise. "You just told a joke. I've never heard you do that before." Nick didn't pay any attention to Mike's teasing and started eating.

"Then, two things happened," Mike continued. "First, the Neanderthals went extinct. They died out. No one knows why, but we know they weren't as smart as modern humans. Second, the climate changed. It got warmer and the glacier began to melt. Modern humans began to move into places that used to be under ice." Nick listened to Mike with interest. "Our ancestors moved up into Europe."

"Are you finally done?" Patrick asked, raising his head. He looked at Nick for the first time. "How are you, Nick?" he asked. Nick nodded to his friend.

"No," Mike answered. "There's more. It was the Stone Age." Patrick rested his head on his hand and crossed his eyes. Mike ignored him and continued. "These people only had trees and rocks, and animal bones and hides to work with. They made lots of really great tools that worked real well for them. They made stone knives and axes. Of course, they made spear heads for hunting."

"Yeah, but I'll bet they weren't smart enough to do math," Patrick teased, continuing to act bored.

"Fred Flintstone has two spears and Barney Rubble has three," Nick began. "If Fred gives his spears to Barney, how many spears does Barney have?"

"You did it again, Nick," Mike said, congratulating his friend on making another joke. "Keep it up and you'll be doing standup comedy." Nick looked puzzled at Mike's comment. He wasn't joking. He was being serious.

"That was their level of math?" Patrick asked wearily. "That's so easy a caveman could do it. No wonder they lived in caves."

Nick grew tired of the string of jokes flowing between Mike and Patrick, jokes that he hadn't completely understood. Changing the subject, he tossed a copy of the local newspaper the Hampton Union on the table. "You guys seen this yet?" he asked.

Mike picked up the paper and looked at the front page. "It's about the Seafood Festival. It happens every September. Tons of tourists come to town to eat chowder and lobster. I've been to it. It's lots of fun. What are you saying? You wanna go?"

"No," Nick said with frustration. "Read the headline down near the bottom of the page."

Battle of the Bands to be Held at the Clamshell, Mike read aloud. "I've been to concerts at the clamshell," he said. "It's that big bandstand right in the middle of the beach, across the street from the Hampton Casino. I've seen some good concerts there. The Air Force band and the Marine band play there every summer. I always wondered how little, old Hampton gets such famous bands to come here."

"Do I have to draw you guys a picture?" Nick asked, annoyed that his friends weren't catching on to his idea. "It's a battle of the bands. The winning band gets an evening on stage at the Hampton Casino. I think we should try to get in. Can you imagine seeing our name, The Sirens, on the Casino marquee? The Casino is famous. It gets major musicians. We would move up to the big time. We could get known as far away as Boston. That's like in another state."

"Nick, the seacoast has lots of rock bands. It has lots of professional rock bands that are well known," Patrick explained. "They're gonna apply and they'll get in. We won't. We'd be wasting our time. We're only sophomores. We just turned 16. A lot of those guys will be in their 20s and 30s and they have big followings. One of those bands will win."

"I'm saying this is a chance at the big time," Nick argued. "We shouldn't miss out because we're too chicken to try. We should apply."

"Let me see that," Patrick said, taking the paper from Mike. "It says we have to submit a demo recording of an original song. We have lots of original songs, but we don't have any of them recorded."

"We can solve that problem," Mike added. "There's a recording studio in Portsmouth. I've been to their website. Recording time costs $50 an hour. I have more than that in my savings."

"So do I," Nick responded.

"Yeah, I do too," Patrick added. "But even if we get in, we get stomped by those professionals. They have lots of fans."

"We don't have to win the battle to get what we need. We would get seen," Mike argued. "We won't get to play at the Casino, but we would get seen by a whole lot of people. You guys have been to the Seafood Festival. It's packed. There are so many people they run busses to bring them in. Nick's right. We probably won't win, but we will get seen, and we get experience. Last year's Homecoming Dance was the biggest audience we've ever had, but we knew most of the people there. They loved us, but maybe it's just because they're our friends, or they graduated from Atlantic Academy and they're being loyal to the school. It's possible other people will think we stink. We should know. It would be a test of how good we really are."

Nick suddenly looked even more worried than normal. "I hadn't thought about that. We'd be in front a bunch of strangers."

"Don't wimp out on me now, Nick," Mike said. "This was your idea. Let's make a list of the things we need to do and decisions we have to make. This is too big an opportunity to mess up. First, we need to get permission from our parents. We'll each be responsible for that one. Remember, they have to agree to let us apply and to spend our money to make a demo. Then, one of us has to contact the lady in charge of the Battle. Her phone number is here in the newspaper. Nick, will you do that? Get all the information you can."

"We need to decide what song we're going to record," Patrick said while Mike added Nick's assignment to the list. "I like The One I'm Waiting For. It's one of our best songs," Patrick added.

"Yeah," Nick added with a smile, an expression that was unusual on his normally serious face. "Everyone thinks it's about a girl. If they only knew it was about being hungry and looking out the window for Bill, the pizza delivery guy." Patrick and Mike grinned at the joke contained in the song. Even though they had written it, they still found it funny.

"We need to decide what to wear," Mike added. "We should all look alike. Dressing alike sends the audience an important message, that we take our music seriously. I think it's a gesture of respect to them too."

"We know the other bands will be wearing, T-shirts and jeans with holes in the knees," Nick replied. "Do we really want to look different from everyone else?"

"Yes," Mike said immediately, without any thought or hesitation. "We want to look different. First, we are different from other bands. Most of them are head bangers and screamers. Second, if we stand out, people will remember us better. That's our reason for going, to get noticed and to begin our own following. We know we're not gonna win." Patrick and Nick nodded. "I'm thinking we should wear our school uniforms." Mike continued. Nick and Patrick raised their eye brows in surprise. Mike added, "Yeah, we should wear our blazers, white shirts and ties. If everyone else is going to be dressed like slobs, we should be as different as possible." Nick and Patrick shrugged in agreement.

"We have to get to Biology," Patrick said, looking at the clock on the wall. "Class starts in five minutes. We can talk more about this later." The three boys walked into the Biology lab and sat in their seats at the big oval table. Mr. LaVallee, the teacher, said he had an announcement. Whatever it was, it obviously pleased and excited him. "Class. I have a special guest today who will talk to us about his work with grain plants," Mr. LaVallee said. He was so enthusiastic he couldn't stand still. He paced back and forth. "I don't know exactly what work he is doing, but he tells me he is making important progress. I want you to meet my old teacher from the University of New Hampshire, Dr. James MacDonald."

Patrick, Nick, and Mike gasped. They had never met Dr. MacDonald, but they had been in his presence, several years in the future when he would announce his discovery. They had saved him from assassination; or rather they will save him from assassination. As they say at the Time Institute, time travel messes with your mind and can make life confusing. They had saved Dr. MacDonald's new-born grandfather from being murdered back in 1901. They had studied the famous scientist during their cadet term at the Time Institute. Their classrooms were in a building dedicated to him, the MacDonald Center. They regularly met in Room 307 in that building when planning missions or being debriefed. In fact, they had blown up the MacDonald Center in the far future. The Dandelions had converted it into a factory to change the earth's atmosphere into their own. Each time they entered or left the MacDonald Center, they touched a bronze plaque honoring Dr. MacDonald. Every cadet did this for luck. The boys knew a lot about this man. Far more than their teacher knew. They knew things the man didn't even know about himself, things that had not happened yet.

Just like at the Hampton Summit, the famous biologist had brought some of his students to Atlantic Academy to assist him. They stood against the wall, ready if their teacher needed their help. Pushing his joystick forward, Dr. MacDonald rolled his electric wheelchair into the classroom. Every time he changed directions, the motor made a loud click. The boys had forgotten that sound. Not surprising. Their first encounter with Dr. MacDonald had been a pretty intense experience. Small details like this clicking sound get lost in a chaotic situation like an attempted assassination. Dr. MacDonald looked the same as he would several years from now, although he had more use of his arms than he would later. When the boys saw him at the Hampton Summit, he could barely raise them to the height of his shoulders. They knew what this meant. In the next couple of years, Dr. MacDonald's muscle disease would destroy even more of his body.

"Thank you for inviting me to speak today, Mr. LaVallee," Dr. MacDonald said to his former student. "Let me tell you a funny story about your teacher," he said to the class seated around the oval table. He winked at them to let them know he was going to tease his friend. "It happened when he was one of my students." Mr. LaVallee blushed. He remembered the incident too. "You all know what a Petri dish is, a small, round plate with a layer of gelatin?" The students all nodded. They had used Petri dishes in lab experiments. "Young Mr. LaVallee was growing a mold for an experiment. He had put the dish in a dark space to allow the mold to grow. When he brought the dish into the light the mold was so disgusting he fainted. His head fell forward and his nose was pressed into the Petri dish. When he woke up he had the mold all over his face. He was so grossed out he had to run to the bathroom to wash. We didn't see him again until the next day." The classroom burst into laughter.

"I hardly ever do that anymore," Mr. LaVallee replied, continuing the joke.

"I thought that would end his interest in biology," Dr. MacDonald teased. "I'm delighted that he stuck with it. In the end, he turned out to be one of my best students." After the laughter subsided Dr. MacDonald began again, "I'm here to talk to you about biology. I hope that like Mr. LaVallee, some of you will consider it as a career. Biology is the study of life, of living things. That's what the word means. It comes from Greek. Bio – life. Logia – the study of."

Mike elbowed Patrick. "Anthropo – Man. Logia – study of," he whispered. Patrick rolled his eyes and shook his head. Nick listened seriously and nodded in interest at this new piece of knowledge Mike had just shared with him.

"Biologists have made life better for countless people," Dr. MacDonald continued. "We have helped cure diseases and provide a better food supply. We have helped clean up the environment. My specialty is grain; those are the hard seeds of cereal plants that humans and animals eat. Wheat, barley, oats, corn, and rice are examples of grains. These grains are often used to make the breakfast food that comes in boxes, the stuff you eat with milk and fruit. These dry foods - corn chex, wheat flakes, and oatmeal -are called cereal, because they are made with these seeds from cereal plants. These grains also make bread and pasta, and lots of other foods.

"Humans have been growing and eating cereals for many thousands of years. It was an important event when people first learned to grow grains. They no longer had to depend on hunting or gathering wild plants. The event changed our development and is so important that it has a name. It's called the Agricultural Revolution." Dr. MacDonald was getting into a subject Mike had been studying in Anthropology, and he listened with interest. "When you hunt and gather food, you have to keep wandering, looking for more. When people began to plant cereals, they could settle down and live in one place. They began to build villages. They created civilization. So, you can see how important grain is. You wouldn't be sitting in a classroom today if our ancestors hadn't started to plant grain." The class nodded. They had never dreamed that what they ate for breakfast was so important.

"The Agricultural Revolution made another important advance when humans noticed that some plants made bigger seeds than others. They saved these bigger seeds and planted them. The result was bigger plants and bigger harvests. They had begun the work I continue. I search for ways to make cereal plants produce more and better grain. This is important because so many people in this world do not have enough to eat. Today, we study plants at the genetic level. I can't tell you too much about some things I'm doing right now. But, I think there may be a way to increase the amount of food we grow. I think we can increase it so much that no one will ever be hungry again. As I said, I can't tell you anymore. My students who work with me and I are very excited by the direction our work has taken. I hope that some of you will think about biology as a career, and that someday you will work with us."

Dr. MacDonald opened the remaining class time to questions. Patrick and Nick didn't raise their hands. They were afraid of slipping and saying something the others must not know. However, they had just learned something important. Dr. MacDonald was working on his discovery several years before the Hampton Summit. He already had an idea of where his research would take him, but at this time, he wasn't sure. They wondered if scholars at UNH and the Time Institute knew this. They made a mental note to share this knowledge with their teachers next time they were at the Institute.

Patrick and Nick didn't ask any questions, but that didn't stop their friend Mike. He was still fixated on the beginning of civilization. He asked, "Dr. MacDonald, you said our ancestors chose to grow plants that had bigger seeds than other plants of the same type? Why does that happen? What makes some seeds bigger?"

"This is caused by genetics too," Dr. MacDonald explained. "Genes explain why some people are bigger than others, or why some have blue eyes and others brown. We get our genes from our parents. Just as tall people are more likely to have tall children; plants with bigger seeds will create more plants with bigger seeds. Sometimes a plant or an animal will be born with an altered gene. This is called a mutation. Because of a mutation an animal may be slightly better at some activity than others of the same species. If that change makes the animal better at getting food, or finding a mate, that mutation is more likely to be passed on through its offspring. Their offspring also become better at getting food, or finding mates.

"Now imagine: generations later another mutation happens, one that makes those animals that are already better at getting food even better at the job. Now, they have such an advantage that they get all the food. The others of the species die out, or move to another place. If that keeps on happening, mutations can result in a completely new species. Of course, this takes a very long time."

"Did that happen with humans?" Mike asked.

"Yes," Dr. MacDonald answered with a smile. It was obvious he was happy this student was so interested in this subject. "The study of humans is called anthropology," the man in the wheelchair told the young high schooler. Mike nodded and held up his anthropology text book. Dr. MacDonald smiled and nodded back. "The same happened with humans. Some mutations resulted in a thumb that made it easier to hold things. This ability was important for making tools. Better toolmakers got more food. Some mutations made it easier to walk on two legs. This made getting around faster, and these people could get more food.

Some mutations resulted in bigger brains and more intelligence. These people could outsmart animals and other humans, and get more food. Do you get the picture?" Mike nodded.

"Did you know there have been many species of humans?" Dr. MacDonald asked. "It took a long time for modern humans to develop." Mike nodded again. "Meanwhile, all the earlier types of humans died out because modern humans got most of the food."

As Patrick and his friends left the classroom their friend Molly caught up with them and led them out into the hallway. Molly was on the Student Council. "We had our first council meeting this morning," Molly said. "We started to plan for the Homecoming Dance. Everyone wanted you to be the band, but Mrs. Martin said that would not happen. She is going to have her brother be the DJ."

"She tried that last year," Nick noted.

"She says that she doesn't know what you did to keep him home, but you won't do it again," Molly said. Actually, the boys had done nothing. Miss Watson had. She and her Fixer team had gone to the man's home and made some minor adjustments to his van. His vehicle wouldn't start until the next morning. In a panic, the Student Council asked the Sirens to play. "Mrs. Martin told us to forget about ever asking you guys to play again. It looks like we'll be stuck with that stupid DJ for the semi-formal and the prom. We all wanted you guys," Molly apologized. She didn't want the boys to think badly of the Student Council and let them know she really would prefer them.

"This year Mrs. Martin isn't taking any chances," Mike said as the boys walked off to their next class.

"Remind me what happened last year?" Patrick asked. "Didn't her brother have trouble with his car? It wouldn't start or something?"

"Yeah," Nick answered. "I'm sure she's gonna make sure he gets here early this time, so there are no glitches."

"Do you guys really care if we don't play at the school anymore?" Mike asked.

"It's the only place we've played," Patrick answered. "I liked it."

"I feel like it's time we stretched our wings and flew this nest," Mike said. "I'm thinking the Battle of the Bands could be our big chance. If so, we're movin' on from good ol' A Squared."

CHAPTER FIVE
BATTLE OF THE BANDS

At 7:00 o'clock on a sunny Saturday morning in mid-September Mrs. Castleton's van was stuck in traffic at Hampton Beach. Slowly, ever so slowly, the van wove its way through a tightly-packed crowd of vehicles. All the other vans, trucks, and cars belonged to vendors, the people who would be selling food, T-shirts, and other souvenirs. The vendors were all trying to get onto Hampton Beach to set up for the Seafood Festival. As soon as a car got to its booth space, the people in it began to unload stoves, coolers, tables, and pots and pans. Then, the car's driver pulled away while the passengers remained to set up their stand. For the next two days at their stand they would be selling seafood specialties or other items. The vendors only had a couple of hours to get ready before the beach road would be closed until Sunday night. By 10:00 in the morning busloads of people would begin to arrive. For the next two days, Hampton Beach would be packed with a milling crowd. It was the biggest event of the year in this small seaside town.

Patrick, Nick, and Mike were crowded in the van with Mrs. Castleton, along with their guitars and drums. Somehow, they would manage to arrive at the clamshell in time to unload, but the van crept along a few feet at a time. It would be a long while before they reached their destination. As they waited the boys watched the activity outside. They also fretted about their performance and their competition. They had paid to have a professional recording done of their demo song. The money they had invested had paid off. The selection committee had accepted them as well as six other bands.

The boys had checked out their competition by visiting their websites, and they knew what they were up against. The guys in these bands were in their 20s and 30s. They all played professionally in clubs and restaurants throughout the seacoast area. They all had fans that would probably show up to vote for them. The kids at Atlantic Academy were the only fans who knew the Sirens. Even if all of them showed up and voted for their school's band, it would not be enough to beat these older bands. No matter, the plan was to get exposure, to become known outside Atlantic Academy.

Mike held a copy of a flyer that had been inserted in the Hampton Union. It announced the Battle of the Bands and listed the groups that would compete. "Shark

Bite, Bleeding Gums, Dog Meat, Toe Jam, The Sirens, Iron Fist, and Swollen Lip," he read out loud.

"Lovely sounding names," Mrs. Castleton said, wrinkling her nose.

"Even our name doesn't fit in," Nick worried. "Bleeding Gums. Dog Meat. The Sirens?"

Mrs. Castleton finally reached the clamshell and Mike and his friends jumped out to unload their equipment on the sidewalk. Mrs. Castleton couldn't get out and help. Cars behind her were already honking their horns to make her move. She wished the boys good luck and rolled on. Nick stayed with their stuff while Patrick and Mike ferried the instruments to the rear of the clamshell. There was a small room off stage where they could wait until their performance. The room had a door that opened onto the stage. When their time came, they would go through the door, set up their instruments, and play.

Meanwhile, the three sat on folding chairs and waited. It would be several hours before the performances began. By then, bus after bus would flow into area and unload tourists who would pack onto the beach. The road through the beach would be closed and tens of thousands of visitors would fill every bit of available space. The boys looked out the door and past the stage. They could see the rows of empty benches in front of the clamshell. They knew those seats would soon fill and the overflow crowd would have to watch while standing.

A while later another band arrived. They were four men, all with long hair and scruffy beards. They wore ragged T-shirts and their jeans had big holes in the knees and in the butts. You could see their underwear. Their arms were covered with multi-colored tattoos. "Hey, little dude," one said to Patrick. "Is this where the bands hang out?"

"Yes," Patrick replied.

"What're you dudes doin' here?" another asked.

"We're the Sirens," Nick answered sheepishly, intimidated by the older players. "We're playing today."

"Ha," another man laughed. "You dudes don't look like rockers. You look like waiters in some restaurant. I mean, like, are those ties around your necks? I don't even own a tie."

Another band arrived. They looked just like the first group – torn jeans, old T-shirts, lots of tattoos. "Hey, man," one musician said to the new arrival. "I haven't seen you since that gig at Maloney's in Newmarket. What you dudes been up to?"

"Yeah, Maloney's. That was a buzz," the man responded. He looked with curiosity at Patrick, Mike, and Nick. "Who are they?" he asked, jerking a thumb at the well-dressed teenagers.

"They're like, that group none of us had ever heard of," a man from the first band responded.

"No wonder nobody knows about 'em," someone in the second group said. "They're kids. Hey, you kids. Where you from?"

"Hampton," Mike replied. He was not happy at the disrespectful way his band was being treated.

"What kinda music you play, dressed up like that?" a man asked. "Are you like a polka band or somethin'?"

At that point a third band arrived. They looked just like the first two, except one of the members did not even wear a T-shirt. He was naked from the waist up. "Hey, Man," one said bending his arm upright and gripping another man's hand, "Cool you're here with us, Murph. We're gonna beat you, though."

"Yeah, like fat chance," the other man named Murph replied. The latest arrival looked at the boys and jerked his thumb at them the same way his predecessor had. "Who are they?"

"They're playing," the man responded. The two burst into laughter. The other bands arrived and joined in mocking the three teenagers dressed in blazers, white shirts, and ties.

We're fifth out of seven," Patrick whispered to his friends. "I wish we were first so we could get out of here sooner. These guys are jerks."

"Weren't they ever a new band? Didn't they start out at some point?" Nick asked. "You would think they would be nicer to the new guys."

As the time for the battle grew closer a crowd began to fill the benches. Soon, the area in front of the clamshell was packed. Mike examined the people through the open door. He was surprised to see so many children and parents. There were even lots of grandparents with gray hair. He smiled slyly. Mike had just noticed something important and he had an idea.

The master of ceremonies walked out onto the stage carrying a microphone. "Ladies and gentlemen," he said in the deep, smooth voice of a professional radio announcer. His voice, made louder by the big speakers, echoed off the buildings across the street from the clamshell. "Welcome to the Seafood Festival's Battle of the Bands. This year we have for your entertainment seven local bands that are competing for your vote. This is how it works. When you paid your admission to the festival, you were given a ballot. Any time today, you can use that ballot to vote for your favorite band. There is a ballot box over here on the left of the stage. There is another as you leave.

"Today, each band will play for a half hour. These are the rules. They will play eight songs. Five have to be original music, written by the band. The other three have to be songs people have heard on the radio, recorded by some other artist. These are called cover songs."

The announcer continued. "This is the prize the winner will receive. They will have an evening at the Hampton Casino Ballroom. The Casino is that long white building right across the street. If you drive through Hampton Beach at six o'clock on a Saturday night, you will see a long line of people over there on the sidewalk. The line stretches around the corner and down the block. Those people are waiting to get into the Casino to see some big name act. You always know who is playing that night, because their name is up on that sign in red lights." He pointed at the Casino marquee. "You, the audience. Your vote will put one of these bands up there in lights.

"I'm sorry, but if you want to come back that night and see our winner, you'll have to buy a ticket to the Casino. But today, it is all free. So, be sure to vote for your favorite band. Now, please join me in welcoming our first act – SHARK BITE!"

A group of men picked up their guitars. Each musician took a piece of the drum set and walked out the door. As they exited, several did fist bumps with musicians from the other bands. Each band member attached his guitar to the amplifiers and strummed some strings. Then, they tuned their instruments. "We're Shark Bite," the lead guitar shouted into the microphone. His voice boomed all over Hampton Beach. Mike watched people in front near the big amps cover their ears in pain. The guitar player began with a screeching, high pitched solo that lasted 30 seconds. Then, the whole band joined in. They were a heavy metal band. The music was loud and the singer screamed so no one could understand the words. He walked back and forth across the stage banging his head up and down, his long hair flying forward and then back with each toss. A half hour later, Shark Bite finished. There was a mild, polite applause.

"What a bunch of stiffs," the guitarist said as he returned to the waiting room. "We warmed 'em up for ya," he said in disgust to the musician named Murph,

73

from the next band. The announcer's rich voice asked the audience to give a welcoming round of applause for the second act, Bleeding Gums. This band wore torn black jeans, black sneakers, and black T-shirts – all but the singer Murph. His chest was bare, exposing a carpet of satanic tattoos. The tattoos on the arms and shoulders of the other members all matched those on Murph's chest, frightening images of demons and skulls. They had smeared dark makeup around their eyes so they looked like ghouls. They all had a lot of piercings in their ears, noses, cheeks, eye brows, and even tongues. If they fell into the water, they couldn't swim, Mike thought to himself. The weight of all that metal would pull them down. The band's songs were dark - about suicide, cutting your arms and legs, and losing your soul. Mike watched as horrified parents stood, took their kids by the hands, and led them away.

Bleeding Gums wrapped up their act and returned back stage. "This audience pukes," Murph the singer said, or more correctly spat. Mike looked out the door and thought, "There isn't much of an audience left. By the time we get on stage we'll be playing to empty seats."

Dog Meat performed next. Their first song – and all the others – were full of obscenities. Mike was right; by the time this band was done few people remained. Toe Jam didn't have any luck getting people to come back to the clamshell. While that band was playing, Mike gathered Patrick and Nick into a huddle. "I want to change the play list," Mike said. Patrick and Nick were stunned that Mike would do this so close to their act. "You know that '60s song we practiced for the really old A Squared alumni? We were going to play it at Homecoming before Mrs. Martin pulled the plug on us." Nick and Patrick nodded. "I want to open with it." The other two protested. Mike raised his hands and said, "Guys, trust me. It's the right song. Being an S/O is about to pay off."

The MC's velvet voice announced The Sirens were playing next. The boys went on stage and set up Patrick's drums and tuned their guitars. Some people near the clamshell saw they were wearing blazers and ties and became curious. This group looked like school boys. They wondered why one wore a captain's hat and his guitar had a wide, hot pink, fuzzy strap. Their curiosity caused them to drift toward the benches.

Mike opened the act singing a song with a driving beat; The kids in Bristol are hot as a pistol, when They-Do-The-Bri-Stol Stomp! It's really something when they join in jumping, when They-Do-The-Bri-Stol Stomp! A shout went up from the crowd that was wandering around the bandstand eating seafood and looking at the other attractions. People began to file into the seats in front of the clamshell. As she walked down one of the aisles a woman with gray hair began to dance the Stomp. A man with gray hair got up to dance with her, just like when they were teenagers. Other grandparents took their grandchildren by the hands and showed them the steps. By the middle of the song dozens of people were dancing in the aisles. Other families began to fill the clamshell, clapping their hands to the strong, catchy beat. Before the song was over, The Sirens were playing to a full house.

"Thank you. Thank you," Mike yelled over the long applause. "Thank you. We are The Sirens from right here in Hampton. On drums we have Patrick Weaver." Patrick played a brief solo and received a rousing applause. "Nick Pope plays bass." Nick played a deep, booming rift and bowed slightly to the excited applause. "And I'm Captain Mike Castleton," Mike yelled as Nick and Patrick began the next song. Mike joined in, singing about waiting for the pizza delivery man; although everyone thought the song was about waiting for a girl. When the Sirens' eight songs had ended, the crowd stood up and applauded. Men put their hands to their mouth and yelled or whistled. Some took off their hats and waved them.

When the Sirens walked off the stage, the audience stood and applauded with energy. The applause continued and continued. Someone yelled "Encore." Soon everyone was yelling "Encore. Encore." The MC looked at Mike, Patrick, and Nick as they stood in the door to the waiting room. "Boys, I think you had better give them what they want, or they'll riot." The Sirens played two encores. After the second Mike reminded the audience there were still two bands left and they deserved their chance to play. The Sirens were finally allowed to leave the stage. By the time Iron Fist and Swollen Lip were done, the audience had drifted away again. None of the other musicians spoke to the boys as they packed up their instruments. They did mumble among themselves and the boys overheard a few words like geeks, and punks.

On Monday afternoon Mike was having lunch with Patrick and Nick in the cafeteria when his cell phone buzzed. He opened it and read the text. It was from his mother. U 1!, it read. Mike wasn't sure what she meant. He showed the message to Patrick and Nick. "You Won!" Patrick shouted, decoding the message. "Call her back and find out if it means what I'm hoping." Mike called his mother, but her phone was busy. He was about to press redial when an announcement came over the public address system. "This just in," Mr. Gibson, the principal said. All through Atlantic Academy's classrooms and halls the students stopped and listened. They could detect the excitement in Mr. Gibson's voice and knew this would be interesting. "Breaking news. Atlantic Academy's very own band, The Sirens, won the Battle of the Bands at the Seafood Festival. It was a landslide! The Sirens are playing in October at the Casino! Congratulations boys. Good job." The cafeteria erupted in screaming applause. A crowd of students gathered around the boys, jumping up and down and slapping them on their backs.

After school, Mr. Newcomb located the boys before they left for home. Mr. Newcomb had been their music teacher when they were in the Atlantic Academy grade school and junior high. Like his descendant, Dr. Newcomb at the Time Institute, Mr. Newcomb wore a perpetual smile. Now, he was grinning from ear to ear. "Congratulations, boys," he said shaking their hands. "The whole school is so proud of you. But, I think I am the proudest." The boys thanked their teacher. It was good to see him again. "Tell me. How did you guys do it? I heard those other bands were all professionals."

Patrick turned to Mike. "It was his idea," he said.

All eyes now looked at Mike, waiting for him to explain his strategy. "I knew the other bands would all look alike," Mike began. "Rockers have a certain look. So, I suggested we be different, so we would stand out. That's why we wore blazers and ties. The other bands made fun of us, but when we got on stage, people became interested. As soon as they saw us, they became curious enough to come back to the clamshell.

"While the other bands were playing I stood in the stage door and watched the audience," Mike continued. "They weren't the same audience you would see at a rock concert - people in their 20s and 30s. They were families. They had old folks with them. They had kids. I realized they found the other bands' music offensive and I knew we should play songs they would like. That's why I opened with Bristol Stomp. I won't do that at the Casino, but I knew we had to play music that fit the audience. That's the mistake the other bands made. They turned off the audience."

"Very clever," Mr. Castleton," Mr. Newcomb said, putting his hand on the younger man's shoulder. "You learned two very important lessons. First, no artist, - no painter, no musician, no writer - ever became successful doing the same thing as everyone else. The great ones are leaders. They are original and creative. They don't copy other people. Other people copy them.

"Second lesson: the relationship between any artist and the audience is always a two-way street. The artist has to create a connection with the audience. You were communicating with those folks. The other bands were playing music at them. You were playing music with them. Never forget that. You and your audience have to be in communication."

"Pretty smart," Patrick said after Mr. Newcomb had left. He punched Mike in the shoulder as a sign of friendship. "You were right. Having an S/O around paid off."

"I just did what they taught me at the Time Institute," Mike explained. "I observed."

Mike Dunbar

CHAPTER SIX
THE NEWSROOM

The Hampton Casino was constructed in 1899 and is a majestic old structure. It is the biggest building on Hampton Beach and is a well-known landmark. Today, the word casino means a place to gamble. However, the Hampton Casino was built so long ago its name comes from the old meaning of the word – a place where people gather for entertainment.

Mike Castleton walked out onto the low stage centered on the Casino's ballroom. He was wearing his captain's hat and holding his guitar, the one with the hot pink shoulder strap. In a matter of hours, the space would be filled with people sitting at small tables listening to his music. Nick and Patrick were waiting back stage, so Mike was the only person in the huge hall, the only person except for three others. Mrs.

Castleton, Mrs. Weaver, and Mrs. Pope sat across the hall at a small table and waved at the young man on the stage.

After winning the Battle of the Bands, The Sirens had run into a minor problem. The Casino served alcohol, and three sixteen year-old boys could not be allowed in unless accompanied by a parent. It didn't matter if those boys were the entertainment; the law is the law. So, their mothers came along for the night. After waving at Mike they left him alone with his thoughts. They knew he was mentally preparing himself for the biggest event of his lifetime, at least so far. He was a high school sophomore and still had a lot of life ahead of him.

Mike scanned the long, wide ballroom, up and down. He had been here last year with his father to see a famous blues musician. The man was so old he played his guitar sitting down. He no longer had the strength to stand through a performance. However, he sure could play that guitar and Mike was in awe of him. Mike thought about the blues player and all the other famous people who had stood on this stage. During the 1930s and 40s world famous Big Bands had set up in the very spot he stood right now. They had played for crowds of dancers that packed the ballroom, night after night. Those bands had played songs they had written and had made famous; songs Mike knew and loved.

Starting in the 1950s big name rock bands had stood right here, right where Mike would stand during the performance that would begin soon. Mike closed his eyes and tried to soak in inspiration from the great ones who had been here before him. He was a time traveler and wondered if some day another young musician who was just beginning his career would stand here and think of The Sirens.

At the end of their performance the Casino audience gave The Sirens long rounds of applause. The band played four encores. By the time people began to file out the boys were exhausted. They dripped with sweat, but they felt good. They had experienced a major success. There was no longer any doubt as to whether or not the public would like their music as much as did the students at Atlantic Academy.

Mike was winding a long cord from his amplifier around his arm when a tall man approached the stage. "Mike," the man said to get the singer's attention. He held out his hand to give Mike the white business card he held between his fingers. "My name is Jay Black. I own a club in Portsmouth named the Newsroom." Mike's eyes opened wide. He knew the Newsroom. All the well-known bands in the seacoast played there. He also knew that all the lesser bands in the seacoast dreamed of a gig at the Newsroom, but it was too exclusive. You had to be invited to play there. Still, bands were always looking for anyone who knew Mr. Black and could put in a good word for them.

"It's a pleasure to meet you, Sir," Mike answered. "I hope you liked our performance."

"I did like it," Mr. Black replied with a smile. "Look, I have a band booked next weekend, but the lead singer has had throat surgery and can't sing. I need to schedule someone else. How would The Sirens like to play for me next Saturday night?"

Mike thought he might faint. He felt dizzy and the ballroom seemed to grow dark. As he began to recover his senses, he thought he was coming out of a dream. No, it was not a dream. Mr. Black really was standing in front of the stage waiting for an answer. Meanwhile, Patrick and Nick had come over to see what was going on between Mike and this man. Mike took advantage of the opportunity to regain his footing. He introduced his band mates to Mr. Black and told them about the offer. They nodded their agreement. "That's it," Mike said. "It's unanimous. The Sirens will be there."

"Great," Mr. Black said, shaking hands with each boy. "Set up at six-thirty. First set at seven. Our standard fee is $2,500 for the night. Just let me know in advance who to make the check out to."

"Did he say $2,500?" Patrick asked as Mr. Black walked away. "He's paying us? I would have paid him to play at the Newsroom."

"I just realized Saturday is Homecoming Day," Nick added. "Mrs. Martin did us a favor. If she hadn't insisted on bringing her brother in as the DJ, we would have already been booked. We would have had to pass on the gig at the Newsroom. Can you believe it? She actually did us a favor."

The next Saturday afternoon, Mike took Menlo for a walk in the woods. He wanted to be alone to mentally prepare himself for the performance that evening. It was mid-October and the leaves had begun to fall from the trees. Those that remained still held a lot of their autumn colors, different shades of reds and yellows mixed in with the last little bit of green. It was a beautiful time to be in a New England forest.

Mike headed for the pond where he and Nick and Patrick used to play when they were younger. Back then, they liked to pretend they were astronauts exploring a newly discovered planet. Now, the boys hid their time craft, the CT 9225 in the woods on the other side of the pond, as no one ever went there. That is where they had seen their first time craft. They had thought it was a UFO. As Mike approached the pond Menlo barked in excited alarm and took off at a run. "You silly hound," Mike called after him, thinking the dog had spotted a squirrel. Menlo ran straight down the path and out of sight around a curve. As Mike rounded the same curve he was amazed to see Allie, Jen, and Lenore on their knees in the newly fallen leaves, hugging and patting Menlo. He had recognized their scent, even before he had seen them.

Mike ran up to the girls, greeting them with as much enthusiasm as had Menlo. He hugged each one, and added a long kiss to Allie's hug. "What are you guys doing here," he asked with a big smile on his face. He was delighted to have his friends with him.

"What are we doing here?" Allie asked with a smile. "What are you doing here? We just came from the Homecoming game and were surprised you, Patrick, and Nick weren't playing. We planned on going to the dance with you again this year."

"Oh boy," Mike began. "This year we're sophomores and would have to play on the junior varsity team. Junior varsity is a lot rougher than the freshman football we played last year. The JV coach wouldn't let Nick on the team. He said JV players would break him like a stick. The team has three quarterbacks who are all juniors, so I would have been on the bench, and Patrick didn't want to play without us. The coach almost cried when Patrick told him. Anyway, we didn't go out for the team this year.

"As for the dance, we're playing somewhere else tonight. Since you guys are already here, why don't you come listen to us?" The girls all agreed enthusiastically. "Oops. Minor problem," Mike said, realizing there would be complications. "Our parents are coming too. This place serves alcohol and we're underage. We'll have to come up with an explanation as to who you are. We can't tell them you're our friends from the future."

Back at the house, Mike's mother was upstairs doing the laundry. "Mom? Some friends dropped by to visit. Can you come down and meet them?" Downstairs Mike introduced Allie, Jen, and Lenore. "They're exchange students," Mike explained. Allie and Jen spoke with slight accents, so the story was believable. "Patrick, Nick, and I know them from the classes we all took together." Mike was pleased. He had managed an explanation that didn't contain any big lies, even though some details were stretched a bit. "Do you mind if they come with us tonight?"

At the Newsroom, Jen, Lenore, and Allie sat at a round table with the six parents. The boys were setting up their equipment. "So, where do you girls come from?" Mrs. Castleton asked, starting the conversation.

"Jen's from New Zealand, and Allie's from Ukraine," Lenore answered. She purposefully did the talking to focus attention on her friends. Lenore was born and raised in Durham, NH, about 8 miles away. However, she wouldn't be born for a long, long time. It would be hard to explain how she had become an exchange student if she admitted she came from Durham.

"My cousin married a man from Ukraine," Mrs. Pope added. "I think he comes from Odessa."

"Odessa is a port city on the Black Sea," Allie explained. "I was raised outside Kiev, the capital. There's a long distance between the two cities. How did they meet?"

After Mrs. Pope told the story about her cousin meeting her husband, Mr. Weaver asked Jen about New Zealand. While Jen was speaking, a waiter came to the table to take their drink orders. "We don't have any money with us," Jen said with alarm.

"Don't worry," Mrs. Castleton said reassuringly, putting her hand on Jen's shoulder. "You're our guests."

The girls weren't sure what to order. They knew what drinks were served in the future, but not in this time. Allie decided to hope for the best. "Do you have Coke?" she asked.

"We only serve Pepsi," the waiter replied. Allie looked at her friends, her eyes pleading for help. Lenore and Jen both shook their heads. They didn't know this drink either.

"What is Pepsi?" Allie asked. The waiter was stunned.

"They come from other countries," Mr. Castleton explained to the waiter.

"Uh, it's like Coke," the waiter told Allie.

"Oh good," Allie answered. "Can I have one?" Jen and Lenore said they would have the same.

"So, where do you girls live?" Mrs. Weaver asked. "Do you stay with American families?"

"We have our own apartment," Jen replied. "We're roommates."

"Oh?" Mrs. Weaver said, surprised that girls at Atlantic Academy would have their own apartment.

"Why do you all dress alike?" Mr. Pope asked, noticing the girls' red Researcher uniforms.

"We're involved with a program at the University of New Hampshire," Allie answered. "They require us to wear these clothes." The parents weren't sure they understood, and there was a pause in the conversation while they wondered what this program could be. Perhaps it had something to do with being an exchange student. They never dreamed the program at UNH Allie referred to was the Time Institute, and it wouldn't exist for generations. Still, Allie's explanation was technically true.

At that moment, Mike stepped to the microphone. He was wearing his captain's hat and his wide, fuzzy, hot pink guitar strap was slung over his shoulder. "Thank you for coming," he said to the audience. The Newsroom was a night club. It was intimate. That means it was a small space with the tables packed closely together. There was only enough room between tables to allow waiters and waitresses to get around. The front row of tables was only a few feet from the low stage where the band stood. The people at those tables were so close they could reach out and touch Mike. As tightly packed as they were, there were far less people here than had been at the Casio or the clamshell. "The band and I decided that this evening we would play only our original music – no cover songs. We hope you like our style." He turned his back to the audience while

Patrick and Nick began the music for the first song. Then, he turned again to face the audience and started singing.

Half way through the first song the audience had fallen silent. The people were not just being polite. In fact, the whole club had fallen silent. Waiters stood between tables like statues. The bartender wasn't mixing any drinks. All the people at the bar had turned to face the band. A lot of the people in the club sat with their mouths open. Some of them had tears in their eyes. This reaction repeated song after song. If Mr. Black had hoped to make money from selling drinks and food, he would be disappointed. No one was drinking or eating. They were all glued to the music.

On the way home, Mike said to his parents, "It's late. Can Jen, Lenore, and Allie stay at the house? They can have my room. Can Patrick and Nick stay too? The three of us will sleep in the living room." That was fine with Mr. and Mrs. Castleton. Mike's mother gave the boys extra pillows and blankets and went to bed. On her way upstairs Mrs. Castleton reminded Mike to let Menlo out and to make sure he was back safely in the house before the boys went to sleep.

"What happened tonight?" Mike asked his friends. "We've played at school, at the clamshell, and at the Casino. We've never had an audience turn to stone on us."

"I don't know," Patrick answered. "They loved us. We got a standing ovation, like we were a symphony orchestra. But when we played, they froze."

"Except for the tears," Nick added. "People were crying. I've never seen so many handkerchiefs. It was like we were at a funeral."

"It happened to me too," Jen added. "I don't know how to describe it. Your music reached inside me and found feelings I didn't know I had. I became so emotional. I'm a Time Institute pilot; I've been trained to remain cool-headed. Tonight, I couldn't. It was like you had this strange power. I loved it, but I couldn't control it."

Allie was the only one who did not talk. She was a music history researcher and knew about The Sirens. She had studied them in school, in the Ukraine. She had written a research paper about them. A lot of mysteries surrounded The Sirens. No one knew why at the peak of their amazing career they had suddenly stopped playing. However, she did know that before they quit they had started a musical revolution. She could not tell the boys anything she knew. She could not risk changing their sequences.

So, she changed the subject. "Guys, we're here for a reason." That got the boys' attention. "We have a mystery at the Institute. We all need to go on a mission to figure it out." She explained what had happened – the island rising out of the sea; the ancient city; the music; the trance. The boys agreed they would go to the Time Institute the next day during the afternoon. They could slip away, do the mission, and be back in time to do their homework for Monday.

The next morning Mike awoke. As usual, Nick was up early and his activity had disturbed his friend. While Nick went to the bathroom to dress, Mike turned on his laptop to check his Facebook page. A little red number at the top of the page said he had 108 messages. It was early on a Sunday morning and already he had more messages than ever before? He wondered if it was a joke, or a virus. Mike checked out the senders. They were all kids from Atlantic Academy. "Check this out," the first message read. It had a link to the Portsmouth Herald's website. "Cool!" was all the second message read. "You guys are famous!" said the next message. "Let me be a roadie," the next friend had written.

Mike followed the link to the newspaper's site. He found himself in the Arts and Entertainment section reading a review about last night. He was surprised. He had not been aware there was a reporter in the audience. "Patrick, wake up," he called to his sleeping friend. "Nick, get back in here." While he waited for Nick, he went to the stairs and called, "Mom, Dad. Allie, Jen, Lenore. Come see." His parents came down in their pajamas. Jen, Lenore, and Allie had thrown on their red uniforms and came down the stairs in a row. Allie's long red hair was all tangled from her night's sleep. Mike made note of this. He had never seen her when her sleek, shiny hair wasn't smoothly brushed. "Wait until you hear this," he said in answer to their puzzled expressions. "You're gonna love it."

Menlo was the last one downstairs. He had gotten up reluctantly and would have preferred to go on sleeping. "So, you slept with the girls last night," Mike said as his dog trotted by, followed by his black and white, J-shaped tail. "One of these days you and I have to talk about loyalty, old friend. You are supposed to be my dog." Menlo ignored Mike and went directly into the living room to where the girls were sitting cross-legged on the floor. He put his head in Lenore's lap and fell back asleep.

With everyone together Mike explained why he had called them. A reporter had attended the performance last night and had written a review in the Sunday morning newspaper. He had the online version on his laptop. "The column is named Seacoast Night Life and it's written by Regina Jones," Mike said.

He began to read the review. "I had the most incredible experience last night. After dinner at our favorite restaurant, my husband and I wandered over to the Newsroom for a drink and to listen to the band Moon Light. It turned out Moon Light's lead singer was recovering from an operation and the band was forced to cancel its performance. Newsroom owner Jay Black surprised the audience by booking a young, unknown band from Hampton at the last minute. We arrived just as The Sirens were taking the stage.

"I didn't feel cheated by the switch. As everyone knows, Mr. Black is very selective in choosing his music. The Newsroom is noted for the quality of the bands he invites. He outdid himself last night. Normally, rock bands sound alike and look alike. Not this one. The Sirens dressed like they were attending classes at their high school, Atlantic Academy. They wore blue blazers, white shirts, and ties.

"However, their music was even more surprising than their age and their appearance. Never has music created such strong emotions in me. I feel pride when I hear the National Anthem. I cry when they play hymns at funerals. This was different. The Sirens' music is audacious and daring. It is not just a listening experience. It's a feeling experience. The Siren's music reaches down inside your heart; it burrows deep into your brain. There, it finds emotions you didn't know you had. I cried, I laughed. I was overjoyed, and I sunk into despair. I was up, and I was down. It turned me inside out. At the end I was exhausted, but I know myself better because the music took my mind to places inside me where it had never been before. The band's name fits them well. Remember the Sirens were legendary mermaids who could hypnotize sailors with their singing. This band does something very similar.

"Mr. Black told me he plans to book The Sirens again. When he does, don't miss them. Soon, people all over the seacoast will be talking about these guys. If you haven't heard them, you will be left out. This band is hot. It has a magic that I predict will take them to the big time. It will not be long before they are appearing at other seacoast locations. Catch them at one of those places if you can't make it to the Newsroom. It will be a night you will never forget.

"The Sirens are made up of three Atlantic Academy sophomores – Patrick Weaver on drums and Nick Pope on bass. Mike Castleton is lead guitar and singer. His signature is a captain's hat and a hot pink, fluffy guitar strap. Mr. Black told me young Castleton writes the songs, both words and music. I don't know if he is a natural talent, or if he learned his skills at his high school. Keep your eye on my column, because I intend to schedule these three guys for an interview. I am just as curious about them as you are."

The people in the living room were silent. It took them a moment to digest what they had just heard. "What was so different about last night?" Mike asked. "We played the same songs at the Newsroom that we played at the Casino. Sure, the Casino audience liked us, but it wasn't like this."

Mrs. Castleton shrugged her shoulders. "I don't know dear, but we are so proud of all three of you. You have come a long way in a very short time. You've worked hard for the past four years to develop your music and you deserve this success. Now, who would like breakfast?"

"We'll help," Jen offered as the three girls stood.

"That will be fun," Mrs. Castleton said enthusiastically. "We'll have girl talk. I live in a house with two men and a dog and I don't get to do that very often." Menlo perked up and ran into the kitchen ahead of the women. He sat in front of the refrigerator door to be there when it opened, just in case anything fell out, or was offered to him.

"I'll make the beds," Mr. Castleton added, as he started upstairs. "Call me when you want me to come down."

The three boys were alone again. They looked at each other. Each hoping the others had some thoughts. At last Mike said, "This reporter is right. We're breaking out. We really could have a shot at the big time. Whether we realize it or not, our lives changed last night. We're no longer the most famous band at A Squared. We're in a much bigger world, and I'm scared. I wasn't ready for this." The others nodded in agreement. This much success, this fast, was scary.

"We can't let our fear overcome us," Mike added bravely, even though he knew he was putting on a show for the others. "We can't let ourselves be surprised again. We need to get ready for what's coming. We need to prepare for the band's future, and even help make it happen."

"What do you have in mind?" Patrick asked.

"We made a bundle of money last night. We should invest it in the band. I say we use the money to buy recording time. We need to record more of our songs. When we have enough, we should produce our own CD. We also need publicity photos. If we had one, the reporter would have included it with her column. Everyone would know what we look like. Seeing a picture would help them remember who we are.

"Allie said the Auckland has a mission it has to do. When we get back, we need to deal with these things. I'm telling you, I have a strong desire to talk with Mr.

Newcomb right now. I have so many questions I want to ask him. I'm gonna send him an email asking if we can have lunch together next week. I'll go over to the grammar school cafeteria to meet him. He knows so much about music. He's helped me before."

That afternoon, the boys and the girls took Menlo for a walk in the woods. It was really an excuse to get away from the house and get about their mission. "We need to take the CT 9225 to its frame of origination and leave it," Jen explained. "You guys fly it there. We'll pick you up and take you to our frame of origination. The CT 9225 will be there waiting for you. The boys climbed into their craft and changed into their gray Fixer uniforms. Meanwhile, the girls got into the Auckland to wait for them to take off. Menlo climbed in with the girls. Mike looked out the CT 9225's door at Menlo. Menlo looked out the Auckland's door at Mike. "Remember that loyalty talk we're going to have," he said to his dog as Patrick closed the craft's door.

Mike Dunbar

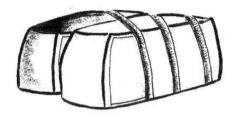

CHAPTER SEVEN
THE GREEN-EYED MONSTER

The boys settled into their apartment in the crew quarters. The Auckland's crew invited them down the hall for supper and then left the boys to go prepare the meal. Menlo went with the girls. He knew food was going to be cooked. If he looked sad enough, bits and pieces would find their way to his mouth.

After supper, Jen suggested the crews begin the mission with a visit to the dig. That way the boys could see it themselves. She knew that Chaz had returned with his team of archaeologists and was already there. Chaz had told the girls about his new plan. He would have his crew work in shifts. No one would be allowed in the trench for more than one day, without taking a day off. Chaz had developed this approach with the doctors at the medical center. He hoped it would allow him to keep the dig going without his people going into a trance.

After supper, the group of time travelers sat together in the Auckland crew's living room and relaxed and chatted. Allie brought out a gift box. The boys looked up wondering what it could be. It wasn't anyone's birthday. Other than the Sirens' success at the Newsroom, nothing noteworthy had happened that would call for a gift. Allie placed the box on the floor in front of Menlo. "Here, this is for you," she told the dog. Menlo sniffed the box and walked around it. Finally, he put a paw on the box and tugged at the ribbon with his teeth. When the bow was untied, he used his nose to push off the box top. He pulled out a piece of clothing.

"What is it?" Patrick asked.

"It's a gift from the Auckland's crew to Menlo," Jen explained. "It was Allie's idea; Lenore drew up the plan. Then, Bashir at the Time Institute laboratory made it. It's a doggy Fixer uniform."

"We all wear uniforms because they identify us as part of the Time Institute," Lenore said. "They protect us if we are lost in space. And they allow us to be invisible on missions. Menlo has accompanied us on the past two missions and he's been a valuable team member. If he can become invisible like us, he will be even more valuable. Also, this will save him if we have an accident in space."

"Look," Allie said with a big smile as she pulled the remaining pieces out of the box. "It has four gloves for his paws and a head cover shaped to his muzzle. There is even a leash. Menlo, you'll be styling." Menlo wasn't sure what all the excitement was about, but everyone kept saying his name and so he joined in. He bounced around the room several times and then went from person to person lapping his or her face.

The next morning the CT 9225 and the Auckland crews packed for their upcoming mission. The first stop was the archaeological dig. The two craft arrived and set down next to the three transports. Those much larger craft were still in the same spot as when the Auckland was here the first time – when Allie stayed with Chaz. Half the archeologists were resting in the camp. It was their day off from the dig. The two crews greeted them and Allie asked if Chaz was in the trench. He was. On the way to the dig, the boys gazed around this new island that was rising out of the Atlantic Ocean. Allie told them that it was even bigger than when she was here. It kept rising every day, and growing.

The crews climbed into the trench. It was deeper now that the archaeologists were working again, and even more of the domed building had been exposed. Allie introduced the CT 9225's crew to Chaz and Will. Patrick, Nick, and Mike were amazed at the size of this building and at its smooth granite construction. The pieces were fit together so exactly the building looked like it had been cut out of one huge block of stone. Buildings in their time, and in the future were not built that perfectly. "How do you think they did that?" Nick asked, running his hand over the polished granite, looking for the joints between blocks. He thought he had found one and put his eye right up to the stone to be sure. He shook his head in wonderment.

"It's frustrating," Chaz answered. "We have no answers. All we have is a great big puzzle."

That evening after supper Chaz invited Allie to go for a walk on the beach. Allie agreed that would be nice, but told him they should invite the others. That wasn't what Chaz had in mind, but he realized it would be rude for him and Allie to go off alone. On the walk Chaz was shoulder-to-shoulder with Allie. He smiled as he talked. He laughed when Allie said something clever. He frequently found a reason to touch her. Mike followed behind with Patrick and Jen. He was miffed that Chaz had cornered his girlfriend and was flirting with her. He was also annoyed that Allie seemed to be enjoying her walk alone with the handsome archaeologist.

While the group was strolling along the beach, Menlo ran himself to exhaustion. This island was flat with no buildings or trees. He could go as far as he wanted without getting out of sight of his people. He had explored everywhere his curiosity had taken him. Now, he had returned and he plodded along side Mike, his tongue hanging out. "It's nice to have you back," Mike muttered to his dog. "You know that conversation we were going to have about loyalty. I think I have to have it with Allie too."

Back at the camp the group pulled folding camp chairs up to the fire. Again, Chaz placed his chair close to Allie's. He continued to smile and laugh and to touch her arm and elbow. Mike sat next to Nick and Lenore and glared at Chaz. "What's with him?" he asked with a pout. "Doesn't he know she's my girl?"

"They became friends when Allie stayed here with him," Lenore explained.

"What?" Mike erupted in anger. "Allie stayed here with him? Were they alone? Where were you guys? How long was it?"

"Jen and I went back to the Institute," Lenore continued. "Allie was here with Chaz for most of a week. Yes, it was just the two of them, but nothing happened. They just became friends."

As a team leader, Patrick realized his S/O was getting overheated. He knew the fastest way to calm Mike down was to distract him with a problem that needed solving. "Hey Brains," he said. "Jen and I have a problem. We need to find this island in the past. We know that no sequences have ever been mapped for it. We need you to develop a plan for us. Join us in the Auckland." The three left together. Nick and Lenore came along to listen.

Mike turned to look back at Allie who was still chatting enthusiastically with Chaz. Menlo was asleep by her chair. "A double slap in the face," Mike muttered to himself. "I've got two traitors on my hands."

In the Auckland, Patrick described the problem they confronted. "How do we find this island in time? Jen and I have checked the directory. Zilch. That was predictable. If there were sequences, this place wouldn't be a mystery."

"Isn't this a job for Mappers?" Nick asked.

"It would be if we had a Mapper team here," Jen replied. "But we don't. We have to do it ourselves."

"I may be able to help," Lenore offered. "We all studied what Mappers do in Rabbi Cohen's History of Time Travel class. But, when I was a cadet, my roommate at the Institute was a Mapper S/O. She explained to me in greater detail how they work. She said a sequence is like driving along a road. A Mapper team gets on the road - the sequence - and follows it as far as they need to go. While driving along, they record all the intersections with other sequences. Then, they go back and map these intersections. So, it's like driving back the way you came, taking a turn at an intersection, and seeing where the next road goes. They do that over and over."

"Rabbi Cohen said Mappers may never finish their work," Mike observed.

"Right," Lenore agreed. "That's why the directory is so incomplete. Sometimes, Mappers bump into sequences that surprise them, that they didn't know where there. They record these accidental discoveries, even though they can't follow them and map them."

"I'm guessing those surprises explain why the directory contains a bunch of sequences that go nowhere," Jen said.

"Yes, exactly," Lenore continued. "My roommate said they don't follow those surprise sequences because getting lost is a major problem for Mappers. It happens to them all the time. The only way out is for the pilot to choose a nearby sequence from the directory and go there. Once they know where they are, they return and start again. It's demanding work."

"My hat's off to the Greens," Patrick said, referring to the green uniforms worn by Mappers. "I'm still asking; how do we find this city in the past?"

"Lenore gave me an idea," Mike said. "What is the oldest sequence in the directory?"

Jen looked it up. "It is a sequence for someone who lived in the corner where France and Spain meet, about 9,000 years ago. It's in there all by itself. It must be one of those accidental discoveries some Mapper team stumbled across. The next oldest is for an Egyptian about 4,000 years ago. It says he was involved in building the pyramids."

"Neolithic," Mike said, thinking to himself.

"Huh?" Patrick asked.

"Neolithic period," Mike answered. "Neo – new. Lithic – stone. It's the New Stone Age. It's the time Dr. MacDonald told us about in our biology class. It's during the Agricultural Revolution, when people started growing their food. They also domesticated animals. This guy probably lived in a village, not a cave.

"Patrick, if you fly to some other place on the planet, will the craft remember its way back to this island?"

"Yeah," Patrick answered. "Piece of cake. All I do is program in this location. We can go anywhere in the world and always come right back to this spot."

"Good," Mike said. "This is my suggestion. I'm figuring that city out there, rising out of the sea, was built before the Egyptians, the Greeks, and the Romans.

If it was around during ancient times, they would have known about it and left us a record."

"This sounds like something Chaz could help us with," Lenore suggested. "He's an archaeologist."

"We don't need him!" Mike snapped. "He can sit out there and flirt with Allie all night long. I know all we need. I'm better at this stuff than he is."

The others in the Auckland were stunned at Mike's angry outburst. They decided it best to let him explain his plan and to not offer any more suggestions, especially ones that involved Chaz.

"First, Patrick, you program in this spot, this new island," Mike continued. "Then, we fly from the island to northern Spain. There, we find the guy whose sequence is in the directory, about 9,000 years ago. Then, we come back to this location, where this island is. We check to see if it and the city are here. If they're not, we go back further in time."

"And how do we do that without any sequences to follow?" Patrick asked.

"At birth, everybody's personal sequence connects to his mother's. We'll start on that guy's sequence. We follow it back until it ends, the day he was born. Then, we pick up his mother's sequence and follow it back to her mother's. We follow a bunch of generations of women's sequences, and then check for the island again. If it's not there, we go back to where we left off. We start following sequences again from mother, to mother, to mother. Then, we'll check again for the island and the city. We keep doing that until we reach the time when the island and the city were above sea level."

"That's going to take a lot of work," Patrick noted. "What if we have to go back a thousand years? That would be a lot of sequences, and a lot of stops to check for the city."

"I didn't say it would be easy," Mike argued. "But, it's the only thing I can come up with. Anybody have another idea?" Every one shook their heads. No, Mike was right. They would have to do it this way. Patrick was right too. This was going to take a lot of work.

"Lenore says Mapper teams get lost all the time," Jen added. "I'm worried about that. They're experienced and know what they're doing. What if one of us gets lost, or if our two craft get separated?"

"We could go in one craft," Patrick suggested.

"It would be safer if we had two," Jen responded. Mike, Lenore, and Nick nodded their heads in agreement. Yes, it was much safer to have two craft. If there was an accident or danger, no one at the Institute would know where, or when, they were. But how to avoid one craft, or both, getting lost?

"I have an idea, Nick announced. "Leave it to Lenore and me. In fact, we should get to work right away." He and Lenore stood up and left the Auckland. "Patrick, we could use a little muscle," Nick said as he walked out the door. Patrick got up and followed the two engineers.

"Mike," Jen said to the Fixer S/O. "You're worrying about nothing. Allie is crazy about you. She's just friends with Chaz."

"She doesn't act like she's crazy about me," Mike pouted. "I'm going for a walk. I'll have to go by myself. Even that dumb dog would rather be with Chaz."

"I'll go with you," Jen offered. "You shouldn't be alone when you're hurting like this." The pair started out for the beach in the distance.

When Mike and Jen returned, they saw the results of Nick's idea. Patrick had helped the two engineers line up the CT 9225 and the Auckland so their sides were touching. Then, he had wrapped them together with dozens of twists of duct tape. When they went on their mission, the two craft would fly together.

"Does one craft have enough power to tow another?" Jen asked.

"No," Lenore answered. "Each craft will be under its own power. You'll be flying the Auckland, and Patrick will be in control of the CT 9225."

"And how is Patrick going to get into the CT 9225?" Jen asked. "His door is pressed up against the Auckland's side."

"We connected his human interface panel into the Auckland's console," Lenore explained. "You'll fly the Auckland like you always do. He'll stand beside you and fly the CT 9225. It will be a bit tricky, but you two are such good pilots we're sure you will get the hang of it fast. We also moved the CT 9225's gear into the

Auckland; since we can't get into the other craft without cutting the duct tape."

"You guys are amazing," Jen said in awe at the two engineers and their work.

"My grandpa always said duct tape will fix anything," Nick announced proudly. "You guys have figured out how we're going to find this city in the past. That means we're ready for this mission. Let's get under way."

Mike was the last one into the Auckland. Jen and Patrick were standing at the pilot's post, in front of their consoles. Nick and Lenore were sitting on one bench holding hands. Allie was on the other bench with Menlo. He had his head in her lap as she gently scratched behind his ear. Mike did not make eye contact with Allie and sat as far from her as he could. She smiled at him and held out her hand for him to hold. He stared straight ahead and folded his arms. Allie's expression showed how much she was hurt and embarrassed. Lenore and Nick looked at the floor to avoid embarrassing her more.

Jen closed the Auckland's door with an addition problem and she and Patrick each started their craft. "Square root two," Jen said. "X plus Y cubed," Patrick added. They had turned on their cloaks. Mike looked up as the two pilots giggled at their math humor problems. Jen showed Patrick her screen and he laughed. Then, he showed her his. She chuckled. "I liked yours better," Patrick told her as he gave her a kiss on the cheek.

"Hold on," Jen told the others. "Northern Spain, here we come. We're going to take it slowly until we get the hang of flying the craft together. We apologize in advance if the ride's a bit bumpy. So, sit back and enjoy." Jen immediately realized she had said the wrong thing. Allie and Mike were not enjoying anything right now.

Jen opened the Auckland's door. Nick and Lenore were seated opposite the door, so they were able to see out. The countryside was green and pleasant. Even before they stood they could feel a soft breeze. "Beautiful," Nick said to Patrick. "How did you ever find a spot this nice?" The hillside overlooked the Atlantic Ocean. A large grove of olive trees spread out below them on the hillside. In the distance, they could see the roof tops of a small village and the masts of fishing boats in the harbor. Here on top of the hill, they were all by themselves.

While the others got out, Jen and Lenore stayed behind to work on the Auckland. "Mike and Allie are having a real tough time," Lenore said to her team leader.

"Yeah," Jen agreed. "I've never seen Mike so angry. I went for a walk with him on the island. He was hurt that Allie was spending all her free time with Chaz. I know Chaz is a nice guy, but Mike is her boyfriend."

"Can you talk Patrick into staying here for a couple of days?" Lenore asked. "It would give them time to work things out. Besides, I don't think we should go on a mission unless our S/Os are working well together." Jen nodded to indicate that she would talk to her boyfriend.

The three girls walked down the hill to the village to buy some food while the boys stayed with the craft. Menlo went with the Auckland's crew. There was no need to cloak. This was their time and they could move about freely. The people in the village knew about the Time Institute and would recognize their red Researcher uniforms. "I know your feelings are hurt," Jen said to Allie as they passed through the olive grove.

"What's wrong with him?" Allie asked with tears in her eyes. "He was fine one minute and then he turned into a monster."

"Well, you did ignore him," Lenore said as gently as possible. "You caused what my grandmother called the green-eyed monster. That's the name she used for jealousy."

"What? When?" Allie asked in surprise.

"Ever since we got to the island," Lenore explained. "You and Chaz spent all your time together and ignored the rest of us."

"Really?" Allie responded. She reviewed the day in her mind. "Yes, we did go off by ourselves, didn't we, on the beach and back at the camp? It's just that we became friends when I stayed on the island. He had so many new things to tell me. The dig is so interesting."

"Oh boy! You S/Os are so smart and so dumb at the same time," Jen told her roommate. "You were so

111

focused on learning about the dig you missed that Chaz has it bad for you."

"Really? No!" Allie insisted. "We're just friends."

"He was flirting with you like crazy and wanted to get you by yourself," Lenore told Allie. "Everyone can see it. Especially Mike."

"I've got some apologizing to do," Allie admitted with concern.

Back on the hill, Mike sat alone on the grass staring at the ocean. Patrick sat on one side of him, and Nick on the other. "Life stinks, eh?" Patrick said to break the ice.

"Yeah," Mike answered. "I have a girl that would rather be with another guy, and a dog that would rather be with that girl. At least I still have you two."

"I know Chaz wants Allie," Nick said. "I don't know why she let him flirt with her all day, but I don't think she's changed her mind about you. Still, you can't treat her like dirt. You have to talk with her and find out what's on her mind."

The boys were still sitting on the grass when they spotted the girls walking up the hill carrying bags of food. They stood up and walked down to meet them. Patrick and Nick took the bags and nodded their heads to Jen and Lenore, a gesture that said come away with us; leave Mike and Allie by themselves.

"I've been a jerk," Mike said. "I'm sorry, Allie. Forgive me."

"No. I need to apologize," Allie answered. "I was the jerk. I spent all that time with Chaz, ignoring you. I should have seen he was flirting with me. I got all wrapped up in what he was telling me about the dig." Mike took her in his arms and kissed her. Menlo wanted in on the hug. He stood on his hind legs, his front paws resting on their shoulders. They each put an arm around the dog and hugged him too. "Mike, I love you so much," Allie said between kisses. "In my daydreams you and I get married. We're from different times and I don't see how it could ever work, but that's what I dream about."

Mike reached into his uniform shirt and pulled out the gold locket that he wore around his neck. "I love you too, Allie," he said looking deeply into the redhead's brown eyes. "Here's the proof. I've never taken this off since the day you gave it to me." He opened the locket and showed Allie the picture Jen had taken of them in the cadet dormitory common room. Just before Jen snapped the photo, Mike had put his arm around Allie's shoulder and pulled her to him. The pair had inclined their heads so they were touching. Allie had given Mike the locket as he left on his first mission. Unsure if they would ever see each other again, she had engraved Remember Me on the inside of the cover, opposite the photo.

"You're the only girl I have ever loved," Mike said from the bottom of his heart. "I wish we could get married. We're both victims of the experience of time. We've got the same problem Jen would have faced if she had married Philip in Alexandria. If we live together in your time, I never grow old. You would age and die and I would still be young. The opposite would happen

113

if we lived in my time. I don't know how we could make it work. I only know I never want to have an argument again."

"I love your dog too," Allie said, giving Menlo a kiss on the nose. "He's so sweet."

"There's no doubt he loves you," Mike said, tugging lovingly on one of Menlo's ears.

By the time Mike and Allie reached the top of the hill, the others had opened the food and spread a cloak cover on the ground. "Welcome back," Lenore said to the lovebirds. "We're having a picnic."

As the group sat eating Mike explained to the others where they were. "The area of ocean out there is called the Bay of Biscay. We're in the corner where France and Spain meet. This is an interesting place. It's called the Basque country. The Basque are an ancient people. Their language is different from all the other European languages. All the other languages – French, German, Spanish - come from a long-dead tongue called Indo-European. But not Basque. No one knows how it got here, or where it came from. It's a unique language. It's not related to any other language in the world."

"Sounds like a mystery for some Research Team," Patrick said, resting back on his elbows. His belly was full and he felt relaxed. Thinking about a strange language was not what he wanted to do in such a beautiful place, on such a beautiful day. He wanted to spend his afternoon with a beautiful woman. He took Jen's hand and put his head on her shoulder. The group fell silent as they all enjoyed the view and the company.

Menlo rolled around on the grass, amusing himself. While on his back, he gently fell asleep with his paws in the air.

The crews camped on the hillside two days. Finally Jen announced, "We have a mission to do. I could stay here forever, but the Time Institute doesn't pay me to hang around." The crews reluctantly packed their gear into the Auckland. "Find that guy's sequence, Patrick," Jen said. "Program it into the CT 9225. I'll do the same with the Auckland. It's amazing he lived right here on this spot, all those years ago. I wonder what his name was?"

"Wasn't it Fred Flintstone?" Nick asked. "Or maybe Barney Rubble?"

"You did it again," Mike teased. "You made a joke. If he hangs around with me long enough, he'll develop a sense of humor," he said to Lenore, while elbowing his friend. Nick smiled. Yes, he had made a joke. He liked it.

Jen closed the Auckland's door and the two pilots answered their math questions. The two craft, tied together with duct tape made a silent, motionless leap 9,000 years back in time. They ended up on a sequence of some unknown guy that some Mapper team had accidentally discovered.

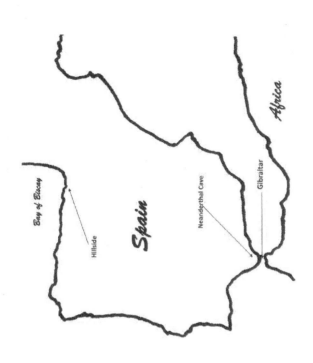

CHAPTER EIGHT
FRED AND WILMA

The Auckland and CT 9225 never moved. They just appeared on the same spot 9,000 years earlier, still bound together with duct tape. The crews put on their gloves and head covers and cloaked. Then, they stepped out to find their man. They were surprised that the scene on the hillside had not changed much in 9,000 years. The olive grove was gone and pine trees grew in its place, but the ocean still sparkled in the distance.

They spotted a young man a short distance away, sitting alone. He was about the same age as the crews. He was dressed in leather clothes and wore jewelry made from seashells and bones. He was looking down the hill and his manner made it clear; he was waiting for someone. The crews soon saw who it was. A young woman was climbing the hill to meet him. She too was wearing leather clothes and the same type of jewelry.

The couple sat together, held hands, and talked while the crews watched. They could not understand the language and were not going to stay in this time long enough to program their helmets. The man put his face near the woman's, looked into her eyes, and said something. The woman burst into a smile and threw her arms around his neck. They kissed awhile. Eventually, the woman stood and pulling on his hand, urged the man to stand. They started down the hill together. All the way down, he had his arm around her and she had her head on his shoulder.

"I wonder what that was all about," Nick said.

"You don't know?" Lenore asked in surprise. "It was so obvious."

"I don't know either," Patrick answered. "She seemed happy though."

"You guys didn't get that? Really?" Allie asked with the same surprise as Lenore. "That was a marriage proposal. He asked her to marry him, and she agreed. They're on the way to the village so she can tell everyone."

"If he is Fred Flintstone," Patrick joked. "We know her name was Wilma."

"Isn't he a little young to get married?" Nick asked.

"If he stays healthy he'll probably live to 35," Mike explained. "If he lives to 50, he'll be a really old man. People in this time have to marry young in order to be around long enough to raise their families." Allie squeezed Mike's hand and put her head on his arm. "He's real lucky," Mike added sadly. "He's got his girl. Even if his life is short, he'll get to live it with her. I'm envious."

The Auckland and the CT 9225 followed the young man's sequence back to his birth. There, his sequence ended and connected to his mother's. The crews exited their craft again and this time found themselves in the village. "Makes sense we'd end up down here," Mike said. "His mother's going to have her baby in her home, not out on the hillside." The crews heard a baby cry in a nearby hut. They knew the young man they had seen propose to his girl had just entered the world. "It messes with your mind," Mike whispered.

With his birth, the man's sequence had just begun. The crews had visited two of his most important frames, being born and choosing a wife. The rest of his life would have to remain a mystery. The crews had a mission. "Okay, that's that," Patrick announced to his friends. Let's pick up his mother's sequence."

"No!" Mike said. "You can't drag me away now. You have to let me see this place. This is what I'm studying in Anthropology. Please, guys. Just a quick look around?"

The village was nicer than the crews would have imagined, nicer than Neo-lithic villages portrayed in the movies. About 100 people lived here. The houses were made of sticks woven together like a basket and then covered with mud. They boys had seen this type of construction before, in Hilton. It's called wattle and daub. The dried mud sealed the walls and kept the wind out. Dogs ran between the houses. Cows and pigs were kept behind wooden rail fences. Fields of grain grew around the village. It was getting near harvest time and waves of high grass swayed in the wind, looking like a green sea.

"They're growing grain," Mike observed. "This is the Agricultural Revolution, just like we talked about in class. Generations ago they noticed that some plants have bigger grains. They've figured out how to get more food from the same ground by choosing and planting just those bigger seeds. Now, harvests are more abundant.

"I need to see their stone tools," Mike told his friends. "This is the New Stone Age. I've seen pictures of their tools in my text book. They were really well made." The group approached a home. A bow and a quiver of arrows hung on a peg outside the door. "This is a longbow," Mike observed. "It is okay, but not as good as the ones we made at Hilton. It is flat on both the front and back. Ours were shaped like the letter D, flat in front and round in back. There's no white sapwood to give it added snap when the archer lets go. This bow is okay for hunting, but not for war."

Mike knew what he was talking about. He, Nick, and Patrick had learned to make longbows and arrows at Hilton in medieval England. The Auckland crew understood. They had learned the bow maker's craft at New Durham in the far future.

"Interesting arrows," Patrick noted. "At Hilton, we made the sticks for the shafts by splitting logs into long, thin pieces. Then, we hammered the pieces through a hole in an iron plate to smooth and straighten them. These arrows look like they are made from shoots of trees."

"No steel arrow heads," Nick said. "These heads are stone, but they're well made. And sharp!" he said testing a point with his finger tip. Pointing to another group of arrows Nick added, "These are interesting heads. They seem to be made from bone. Why do you think they have these strange teeth on the edges? They look like some sort of comb."

"Those are for fishing," Mike explained. "Those curved teeth that bend away from the point are called barbs. Once the arrowhead goes through the fish the barbs hold it like hooks. No matter how much the fish squirms, it can't pull loose. See these arrows with a round stone head? They're made for shooting birds. The arrow doesn't go into the bird; it just hits it hard, like a punch. It knocks the bird out of the air so the hunter's dog can get it."

Mike waved to his friends to follow him. He had found what he was looking for. He approached a group of three men from behind. They were sitting on the ground making stone tools. They started by hitting a rough stone with a smooth, round stone. The blow broke the rough stone into smaller pieces. "This is called flint knapping," Mike explained, whispering through his helmet radio. The others could hear him, but the men could not. "My Anthropology teacher showed the class a video about this. The video showed some guys from our time who have figured out how flint knapping was done. The round stone is a hammer stone. It breaks the flint into pieces. This guy is shaping the pieces with a deer antler. He presses on the flint and small chips slide off. He does that until he gets the shape he wants."

"What is that man making?" Lenore asked. "The one putting pieces of flint into a curved stick."

"It's going to become a sickle," Mike answered. "It's a tool for cutting grain when they bring in the harvest."

"Seen enough?" Patrick asked Mike. "We do have a mission."

"Yeah, thanks," Mike answered. "I'm ready to go." On the way out of the village the group stopped one more time to watch a group of woman grinding flour. They were using round stones the size and shape of a submarine sandwich. They put a handful of grain on a flat rock and crushed it by rolling the round stone over it. This turned the grain into flour. The women swept the white dust into a clay bowl and started on another handful.

"Peaceful place," Mike said as they returned to the craft. "This village reminds me of Hilton, New Durham, and Kwaisiton. It's nice - living in a small town where you know all your neighbors and work with them."

The two time craft picked up the man's mother's sequence and followed it back to her birth. When they opened the Auckland's door the crews were surprised to find themselves in a different village. "Of course," Mike announced. "The women are born in one village, but usually marry a man from another village. Then, as a new wife, she goes to live with her husband. It makes sense. Their villages are so small everyone is related. If you're a girl, your choices of a husband are pretty limited. Most of the men in your village are either your cousins or your brothers."

"Ooooo!" Jen said twisting her face like she had eaten a lemon. "I have two brothers. I wouldn't want to end up married to either of them. My cousins aren't so great either."

"Yeah," Allie agreed. "I have a brother too. The thought of marrying him gives me the creeps."

"You have a brother?" Mike asked. "I didn't know that."

Next, the crews jumped to the mother's mother's sequence. Then they followed her grandmother's, and then her great grandmother's. Lenore, Mike and Allie, counted five sequences and recorded them for the directory.

After five sequences Jen and Patrick flew the craft over the ocean to look for the island and the unidentified city. They were not there – just wide, rolling sea. "The rest of the world is still in the Stone Age and that incredible city has already come and gone," Allie said. "They're going to have to rewrite the history books. Chaz has an amazing discovery on his hands." Mike scowled at hearing his girlfriend mention the archaeologist's name.

The crews repeated the same search pattern over and over. They followed the sequences for five mothers and each time, ended up in a new village. This happened so many times, they were no longer sure where they were. Perhaps they weren't even in Spain any more. Mike figured they had gone back 600 years.

"I'm beat," Nick said at the end of a sequence. "We've been working all day. When do we knock off? Come to think of it, we haven't been working all day. We've been working for six centuries. I'm tired."

"It is curious," Lenore added. "We're tired from all this work. But because we have been jumping around in time, we have no way to measure how many hours we've been at it. I guess we just have to listen to our bodies. We should quit when they tell us that we've done a day's work. Time travel sure does mess with the mind."

The crews examined the forest around the craft to be sure there was no danger. Then, Patrick and Mike gathered some wood while Nick started a fire. As the sun went down Mike advised, "We should go into the craft. This is the Neolithic and there are lots of wild animals roaming around. They're all extinct in our time. But they are here now, and they hunt at night. I'm too young to become someone's dinner."

"They would take Patrick first," Nick replied. "He has more meat on his bones."

"Good job, Nick," Mike congratulated his friend. "You just made another joke." Nick was surprised. He wasn't trying to be funny; he had just said the obvious. If you were an animal looking for someone to eat, Patrick was a better choice than Mike. He had more meat on his bones.

It was cramped in the craft. The sun had set, but it was too early to go to sleep. The crews were bored, cooped up inside the tight space. "I wish we had a television," Patrick said. "Or a CD player."

"That reminds me," Mike told Allie. "I brought something to show you." He rummaged around in his bag and found a small box-shaped device. "It's a Pitch Perfect," he told her. "It's a technology that's being used a lot by singers in my time. It adjusts a singer's pitch. If his voice is flat, or he can't reach a note, this takes care of it for him. No matter how bad he is, he sounds perfect."

Allie said, "I read about this technology when I was in school in Ukraine studying music history, before I became a cadet. Don't I remember that a lot of people didn't like it? They thought it was wrong for singers to use it"

"I'm one of them," Mike answered. "I think this technology is cheating."

"How does it work?" Allie asked.

"The microphone plugs into this jack on this end," Mike explained. "The amplifier plugs in here on the other end. The voice goes in one side and comes out the other. If it's off key when it goes in, it comes out all adjusted and perfect. The audience hears the song with no mistakes."

"If you think it's cheating, why did you buy one?" Nick asked. He reached over and took the Pitch Perfect from Mike.

"I thought I should know how they work," Mike told Nick, while his friend examined the device. "I would never use one in a performance. That's lying to the audience. If a performer can't sing all the notes, he or she shouldn't sing that song. The Pitch Perfect is like an athlete using performance enhancing drugs. The guys who take drugs can do things they couldn't do before. It's cheating. When my audience hears me sing they have a right to know the voice they hear is me, the way I really sound."

Nick opened the Pitch Perfect's case and looked inside. "Hmm," he said, showing the electronics to Lenore. "This is how it works." Lenore looked inside and nodded her head. She was an engineer too and figured out the gadget as fast as Nick.

"It's lights out, guys," Jen announced. "We have to get some sleep. I hope we get lucky tomorrow and find that city right away, but I'm afraid we still have lots of work ahead of us." The two crews were cramped in the Auckland. They spent a long time shifting around the crowded cabin trying to find a comfortable position. Allie and Lenore were the smallest, so they slept on the bench seats with their knees pulled up to their hips. The other four twisted and squeezed themselves so they all fit on the floor like pieces to a puzzle. Menlo tried to find a spot on the floor, but gave up. He walked over the four bodies and jumped up with Allie. She wrapped her arm around him so he wouldn't fall off the bench seat. In minutes, Menlo began to snore.

Jen woke up with Nick's foot in her face. She struggled to pull herself into a standing position so she could look out the porthole windows. There was no danger. She opened the Auckland's door and stepped out. "Up and at 'em, you guys," she told the sleeping crews. "We've got a full schedule ahead of us." The crews joined Jen outside and stretched the kinks out of their stiff bodies.

The six time travelers and their dog picked up where they had left off the day before. Mike and Allie kept track of how many generations they jumped backwards in time. While they had no way of knowing what year it was, it was important they make a good guess. To do his work, Chaz needed to know the city's approximate age. With Lenore's help, Mike and Allie logged each woman's sequence. When they got back, they would give their records to the Institute to add to the directory.

Mike observed the tools and clothes people wore. They changed as they moved back in time, and were no longer as well made as in the Neolithic village. "It makes sense," he explained to the others. "Human progress happened as time moved forward. We're moving backward, so we're seeing change happen in the opposite way. Things are going from more advanced to more primitive. At some point, we're going to end up in the Old Stone Age."

The next time the crews got out of the Auckland they found themselves outside a cave, rather than in a village. Smoke was rising from the cave's opening and people were working inside and out. There was snow on the ground. "It's happened," Mike said. "These are cavemen. We've gone back before the Agricultural Revolution, the time when people started living in villages."

"I've noticed that the air has been colder the last several sequences," Lenore said. "Why do we keep stopping in winter?"

"Until about 10,000 years before our time most of Europe was covered by a glacier," Mike explained. "It was a sheet of ice 3000 feet thick. That's like ten football fields stacked end on end. The pack of ice was huge. The climate was so cold people moved south looking for places warm enough for them to live. They ended up in southern Spain and Italy. I'm guessing we're in one of those places. Those countries are warm in our time, but their temperatures were much lower during the glacier. That's why it gets colder the farther back we go in time. Unless we find that city soon, it's gonna get worse. Right now, the Ice Age is ending and things are warming up. We're going back into it. The weather will get a lot colder."

After their long search the crews were tired and decided to spend the night in the woods near the cave. Once again, they crammed themselves into the Auckland's cabin. The next day, they continued their search. They followed women's sequences and traveled back into the Ice Age. Mike was right. They saw more and more snow and it got colder and colder.

As they stood outside another cave Mike informed his companions they were definitely in the Old Stone Age. "You guys have to let me look around again," he begged. "This will help me so much with my Anthropology class."

The cloaked time crews snuck into the cave and watched the inhabitants go about their lives. There were a lot fewer people in this group of cave dwellers than in the Neolithic villages. Mike explained that these people were still modern humans; they just had a more primitive technology than the villagers. The cave residents did look like people you would see back home on the street, except they wore skins and the men had beards.

The people had dogs, but no cows or pigs. Mike showed his friends their tools and weapons. The cavemen had bows and arrows and spears. Their stone knives were primitive compared to what they had seen in the Neolithic village.

Talking through his helmet communication system so the cavemen would not hear the invisible visitors, Mike called the others to come see something he had found. "You have to see this woman," he said. The woman was lying on top of an animal skin and seemed to be sick. One of the cave women was feeding her. "She looks different from the others," Mike said. The time travelers all agreed. She did appear different from the other cave dwellers. She was short and heavy. She had thicker arms and legs. Her forehead was bigger and her nose was wider. Her hair was a sandy red, her eyes were blue, and her skin was fair. All the others in the cave had dark hair, brown eyes, and an olive skin.

"Do you know what she is?" Mike asked the others with excitement in his voice, like he had made an amazing discovery. "This woman is a Neanderthal! This is amazing. I figure we're gone back about 12,000 years before our time. My text book said Neanderthals lived in southern Spain and went extinct about 24,000 years before our time. This woman shouldn't be here. But she is. This means Neanderthals lived a lot longer than we thought.

"I'm not sure why she's here in this cave with a bunch of modern humans," Mike added.

"They're caring for her," Allie said. "I wonder if they found her sick and took her in."

"That's as good a guess as any," Mike replied. "Compassion is a trait of modern humans." The group left the cave and returned to their craft. Before boarding to continue their search Mike pulled off his head cover and said to the others, "If they have a sick Neanderthal in there, that means there must be more of them in this area. We have to find them."

"Mike, so far we've put up with your fascination with all this anthropology stuff and we haven't complained," Patrick said. "I'm tired. I'm tired of following sequences. I'm sick of squeezing into a crowded craft. I want to find that city for Chaz. Then, I want to go back to the crew quarters. I want to take a shower, have a good meal, and sleep in a bed."

"Guys," Mike argued. "We have to find the Neanderthals. We've made a major discovery. Isn't that our job? The reason we time travel is to learn new things, to increase knowledge."

The others looked at the ground. They all felt like Patrick. They were tired. This mission was wearing them down. However, Mike was right. They time traveled to expand knowledge. They had stumbled onto something important, and they had to do their job. "Okay," Jen said to the crews. "All aboard. What's your plan, Mike? How do we find a tribe of Neanderthals without a map?"

"We do the same as when we were looking for the Auckland outside Carthage. Fly in an outward spiral. It's pretty safe to say the Neanderthals live in a cave. They have to be burning a fire for heat, as it's too cold to survive without one. We should be able to spot the smoke, even at a long distance.

Mike was right. Spiraling outward Jen and Patrick spotted a cloud of smoke coming up from a hillside. They set the craft down outside another cave. The crews cloaked their uniforms so they could sneak inside. Like the sick woman, these were Neanderthals and they were all short and muscular. Mike led the others around the cavern. He showed them how differently Neanderthals lived from the modern humans in the other cave. Things were really primitive here. The Neanderthals didn't have bows and arrows. They only had stone-pointed spears. There were no dogs. There were only a few children. "They're going extinct," Mike said. "Without children, there will soon be no Neanderthals. We've arrived real close to the end of their species."

The crews left the cave, and before going the craft stopped to look at the scenery. "I recognize that shape," Patrick said, pointing at a large hill standing all by itself. It's the Rock of Gibraltar. You see it in ads for an insurance company. Where's all the water? Gibraltar stands in the middle of the sea."

"You're right," Mike replied. "That is Gibraltar. I recognize it too. That means we're in southern Spain. There's no water around the rock because the oceans are so much lower. Remember, a lot of the earth's water is locked up in that enormous glacier. If we walked in that direction we would end up in Africa. You can't do that in our time, because there's ocean between Africa and Spain. Now we now know where we are. Since we left that first Neolithic village, we've gone south. Makes sense that we would move from the cold north to a warmer area."

"You've found your Neanderthals, Mike," Jen said. "We still have our mission. Now, can we look for the island and the city?"

The Auckland and CT 9225 headed out to sea, to the location where the island and the city should be. The two crews were surprised when they came to land. Every other time they had flown over this area had only been ocean. "I think we have finally found it,"

Nick said. "Only this island is a lot bigger than that one Chaz is working on."

The two crews saw the city in the distance. They couldn't miss it. Even from far away, the polished granite was beautiful. The city sparkled like a crown covered with colored jewels. When they reached the city Jen and Patrick flew low over the buildings. The time travelers were amazed at how perfect everything looked. The city was clean and neat. It was like it had just been built and no one had moved in. "Let's fly around for a while," Allie suggested. "We should get an idea of what's down there before we land. It looks pretty quiet from up here, but there could be danger."

Mike Dunbar

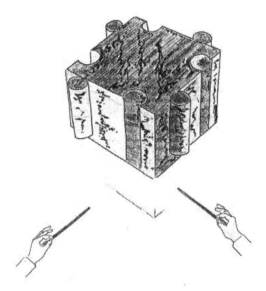

CHAPTER NINE
ALAYNIESS

"Our first job is to program our helmets," Mike said. "Once we do that, we can communicate with the people in this city – if we ever find any. I don't see anyone."

"Let's fly toward the dome," Jen suggested to Patrick. "Chaz said it was an important place. I would expect to find people there." The two time craft banked into a curve and flew off toward the yellow dome. Jen was right. There was a crowd at the dome, but they were not acting like people going about their daily business. Some inhabitants did appear to be working. A small group was involved in moving a large granite block that looked like a piece to a huge, three-dimensional jigsaw puzzle. However, there was no heavy equipment to do the moving. Other people were working on three huge statues that stood in a row. All the rest were standing still, doing nothing. That is precisely what they were doing – nothing, nothing at all. In fact, they were not even moving. They were frozen in place.

As Jen and Patrick landed the craft the crews donned their head covers and gloves. Allie got on her knees in front of Menlo and dressed him in his uniform. The dog liked the attention. As Allie worked he kissed her repeatedly, returning her attention. When Allie was done she pressed a switch on Menlo's chest, and he disappeared. "Bashir put a switch in Jen's remote, so she can turn Menlo's cloak on and off at a distance," Allie told the others. Then, she used her hand to wipe her cheek and chin where she had been kissed repeatedly.

The cloaked crews exited the craft. As they approached the people in the square they found lots of things to amaze them. Nick and Lenore were fascinated by the work that was being done. The huge block of granite was being moved by people standing at its corners holding some sort of rod. The block was defying gravity. It floated slowly along, apparently controlled by the rods. "This technology is way beyond anything we have," Nick said in awe. "In my time, we would use a crane to move that block. In the future, they use reverse gravity polarizers, like in our time craft. That's not what these people are doing. I wish we could take one of those rods into the Time Institute lab," he said to Lenore. "We would have fun taking that apart." Lenore nodded as she admired the technology and thought the same thoughts as Nick.

"Can you imagine the mathematics they used to figure out that block's shape?" Jen asked Patrick as she stared at the complicated piece of polished granite. That's exactly what Patrick was thinking. "We would have to use computers to create that shape," Jen added. "Wouldn't you love to sit down with one of their text books?"

Allie examined the people and noticed they were all about her size. She was used to being with people her height. All the time crews and many of the Institute's teachers were small, but there were also larger people there, and at UNH too. Here, everyone was about five feet tall. The tops of their heads only came up to Nick's shoulders.

Mike looked at the buildings around the plaza and thinking aloud said, "This shouldn't be here. The rest of the world is still in the Stone Age and living in caves. This shouldn't be here. Who are these people? Where did they come from?"

Continuing to examine the men and women in the plaza, Allie elbowed Mike. "Look at their faces," she said. The others heard her and turned to see what Allie had noticed. The people had no expression. The workers watched the block as it moved. However, their faces were blank. All the other people in the square stood perfectly still. They were not watching the work.

They stared straight ahead. Their arms hung at their sides and there was no expression on their faces.

"Are they robots?" Nick asked

"I'll check it out," Patrick said. He approached a man, and more closely than anyone would find comfortable, examined the man's face. The man could not see the invisible time traveler just inches from his nose, and did not react. Patrick watched a while longer and observed the man blink. He looked at the man's chest and could tell he was breathing. Otherwise, the man, and all the others stood as still as statues. "He's human, not a robot," Patrick told the others after examining the man. "But it's like no one's home."

Nick and Lenore turned their attention to the three enormous statues that were being carved, and tugged the others to follow them in that direction. They were amazed as they watched the carvers use their rods to slice away chunks of granite. To do so, they pointed the rod at the huge block of stone. Without any blade, without any beam, the rock was sliced off, leaving a surface as smooth as glass. No polishing was required. The carvers lowered the cut-away granite with the same rods. He or she pointed the rod at the sliced stone and it slowly lowered to the plaza, under complete control. "Amazing," Nick muttered to Lenore. "I have to take apart one of those rods. I just have to."

"Guys," Patrick announced. "This all very interesting, but there is a big problem. We need to program our helmets. To do that, we have to leave them someplace where people are talking. There are lots of people here, but is no one is saying anything. We have to find another location."

The crews climbed back into the Auckland and the two craft took off. "Any ideas," Jen asked the others. "Where do we find people who are not doing a robot imitation?"

"Let's do the outward spiral," Patrick suggested. "We'll cover most of the city that way. If there is any place where people gather and act normal, we'll spot them."

"I can't believe how big this city is," Lenore noted after the craft had been flying for a while. "It goes on forever." It did extend a long way, but not quite forever. Eventually, the Auckland and CT 9225 reached the edge. Outside the city, the craft began to fly over farmland. "We have even less chance of finding people gathering and talking out here," Lenore said.

Eventually, the two craft reached the ocean. "This land is a lot bigger than most islands," Mike noted. "It's like a small country. Let's fly along the shore and see if we can find a harbor and some boats. Where there are sailors, there are taverns. Where there are taverns, people gather and talk."

The time travelers did not come to a harbor, but they did find a large building standing in the middle of nowhere, all by itself. It was all by itself in the sense that there were no other buildings. However, there were lots of people, and they were moving, not standing like statues. They had set up tents and small shelters. This told the crews that they were camping in this place, not passing through. "I think we just found what we're looking for," Jen announced. She and Patrick set the craft down behind some trees.

"Mike, you and Allie are the best ones for this job," Patrick told the two S/Os. "Find a place to leave our helmets, and then put to use your astounding powers of observation," he added jokingly. "Find out what you can. Anything that will help us."

"Menlo, stay with Lenore," Mike told his dog. Menlo jumped up on the bench seat and sat next to Lenore. She put her arm around him and he lapped her cheek. The two S/Os cloaked, stepped out of the craft, and walked toward the building. People were standing or sitting in groups talking. Others dozed on the grass. There were so many people the cloaked S/Os had to work at avoiding them. "What do you make of this?" Mike asked Allie through their head cover communicators.

"They're camping. It's a picnic, or maybe a meeting of some sort," Allie answered. "They don't seem to be doing any work." As the two invisible time travelers entered the building Allie said immediately, "We know what this is. We saw lots of them when we were cadets and taking our Methods of Observation class."

"Yeah, Mike answered. "There's no doubt. It's a temple. In fact, there's the altar. It's in front of two statues of gods." The statues were huge and carved from the same yellow granite as the domed building. They represented a man and a woman standing side by side, holding hands like they were in love. The statues stared out to sea, out to the east where the sun would rise every morning. Gifts and sacrifices were piled in front of the statues. "These people are pilgrims," Mike said. "They've come here on a pilgrimage to worship."

Inside the temple was not a good place to leave the helmets for programming. There were lots of people in the building, but they were all praying silently. "We have to find a place outside where people are talking," Allie told Mike, jerking her thumb toward the campground. Outside, they spotted a ledge over a window. Plenty of people were sitting on the porch under the window and the helmets could hear them clearly.

Mike put his hands together and Allie placed her foot in them. Then, he boosted her high enough to place the helmets on the ledge. Allie covered them with a craft cloak cover so they would not be seen. Then, she tapped Mike on the head to tell him she was done. He slowly lowered her.

Back in the craft, Nick announced, "I can't want to wait in this cabin for three days. It's too cramped. I'll go nuts. I vote we do some exploring while the helmets are being programmed." The others all nodded in agreement. This huge island was in the tropics. Even though the earth was beginning to come out of an ice age, and the glaciers were melting, it was warm and pleasant here.

"These people are camping, so it must be safe to sleep outside at night," Patrick observed. "I guess that means there are no wild animals in the area. It should be safe for us too. We have Menlo just in case. He'll warn us if there's any danger."

The crews followed a footpath away from the temple and came to a road. They followed the road to the west, away from the ocean, and found themselves in farmland. Crops grew in small, neat fields on both sides of the road. There were no farm animals. In fact, birds were the only animals the crews saw on their tour. Nick made the group wait while he watched a farmer working. The farmer was holding a rod parallel to the ground. As he slowly walked along his field, the grain in front of the rod fell like it was being mowed. Another farmer followed behind the first, holding another rod. As he walked along, the grass swept itself up into long rows. "They are using those rods to harvest the grain," Nick told the others in awe. "I have to get my hands on one of those things."

Three days later, after making a long loop through the countryside, the crews ended up back at their craft. The others watched while Mike and Allie found the helmets and returned them to their friends. "We need information," Mike said. "This mission is one big mystery, both now and in our time. One option is to cloak and just listen to these people talk. Maybe we will learn some things. But we can't be sure they will answer our questions. There is no point in going back to the city. No one there is talking. I suggest the second option. We uncloak and introduce ourselves to these people. They seem friendly."

"That's too risky," Patrick said. "They look friendly, but what if they're not? This is my idea. The girls are the same size as these people. They will fit in better than we will. Nick, you're so tall you'll give them heart attacks. We'll stay cloaked, but we'll stand right beside the girls. If there are any problems, we jump in and rescue them. We're so much bigger than these people; we can fight our way back to the craft. I don't think we'll have any trouble here, but if we do, that's our fall back plan."

"You do the talking, Allie," Jen said. "With your bubbly personality you can start a conversation with a statue." Jen was right. Allie could chat with strangers and make them feel comfortable. When they were cadets at the Institute, there was always a crowd around Allie. She was the best one to approach these people.

All six donned their programmed helmets and the boys cloaked. The three girls approached two men who were sitting on the porch talking. "Hello," Allie said. "It is a very nice day."

The two men looked up with surprise on their faces. "Yes," one replied to Allie. "It is very nice." He paused. "I have never seen people like you. I have never seen hair your color." Allie's long, silky hair was auburn red. To Jen he said, "I have never seen eyes your color." Jen's eyes were a smoky gray. To Lenore he added, "I have never seen skin your color." Lenore's skin was like rich, smooth chocolate.

"Where are you from?" the second man asked.

Allie and the girls studied the men and then glanced at the other people gathered around the temple. She was slightly embarrassed she had had not noticed before. All these people had wavy brown hair and brown eyes. So yes, the three girls were different from these pilgrims. Allie's embarrassment turned into irritation with herself. She was an S/O and observing such important details was part of her job. Although invisible, Mike was silently embarrassed as well. He asked himself how after all his training, he had not noticed something this important.

"We are explorers," Allie replied. "We have come from far away."

"Where could you come from?" the second man asked with curiosity. "We travel all over the world to obtain different types of granite. We know there are people in the lands to the east, across the sea. There are two types, the tall, dark slender ones, and the short, fair heavy ones. Both types are primitive. They live in caves and hunt animals. They use long sticks with sharp stones attached to the ends. They wear skins." The girls realized the man was talking about the Neanderthals and modern humans. "You cannot be from those people," the man added. "You wear clothing. They don't know how to make cloth. We don't know of any other people on earth. Where do you live?"

Allie knew she couldn't tell them about New Hampshire. The state's nickname is the Granite State. These people had probably been there gathering granite. She changed the subject. "What is this place?" she asked.

"This?" the first man asked, pointing to the temple behind him. "This is the shrine to the Loving Couple, the god Alaynius and his consort Alaynia."

"What's a consort?" Patrick whispered to Mike.

"His wife," Mike whispered back.

"The god and his consort face east," the man explained. "Each morning they greet the morning sun. The sun and the earth are their creation. They stand here in love, to admire and bless their creation as each day begins. We are their children. They gave us this good earth. They placed this great land in this spot on this world. The Loving Couple placed us directly under the sun so we would be warm, even as the rest of the world is covered in ice." The girls knew what he meant. His land was on the equator, so the sun was straight overhead every day.

"We are pilgrims," the second man added. "We are here to pray to the Loving Couple to remove the curse from our land - to save our people. We worry that we have sinned, that we have brought this punishment on ourselves. We pilgrims pray day and night. We are on a rotation. So, every minute of the day some of us are in the temple. Our prayers never stop."

"When I asked what this place is," Allie continued. "I meant this huge island and the city."

The men were shocked at the question. The look on their faces revealed what they were asking themselves. How could anyone not know that city?

"This land is named after our gods," the second man said. "The city is named after our land. This land is Alayniess. The city is Alayniess – the Eternal City." At last the crews had learned the city's name. It was Alayniess. It wasn't much information, but it was important.

While tracing the cave women's sequences the crews had flown over this patch of ocean many times. In the future, they had seen only water. That meant that sometime after this visit, the city had sunk into the sea. From their search, they knew roughly when that disaster was going to happen, in less than five cave-woman generations, sometime in the next 100 years. Could these pilgrims at the temple know this? Is this the curse they had mentioned?

"We visited the city," Allie said. "It is beautiful."

"You have been in the city?" the first man asked in shock. "How did you get out?" It was Allie's turn to not understand a question, and that showed in her expression. She had no trouble leaving the city. "Everyone in there is in a trance," the man explained. "We do not go in there. Anyone who stays there for two days never comes back. Some have gone in and got out immediately. They have told us what they saw. All the people in the city have lost their will and their awareness."

"That's the answer," Allie explained. "We did not stay long. However, we did see the people in the trance. Tell me, what do you know about this trance? What causes it? When did it begin?"

"We know very little," the second man replied. "We don't know what causes it, only that it takes about two days to happen. It began about six months ago, during the most recent consulate. The consuls had been elected about a year earlier."

"Consul?" Patrick whispered to Mike.

"It's a political position, like a president," Mike whispered back. "The difference is that there are usually three consuls, not one."

"We who live out here in the country don't get as much news as the city people," the first man added. "We heard that under the new consuls life in there was good, as it had always been. The only change is that the consuls gave themselves a name. They started calling themselves the Triumvirate. People thought that was a strange title. It seemed too proud. Our elected leaders have always been humble servants of the people. It is an honor to be elected. It is an honor to serve."

The man second man continued, "There was another interesting thing. The singing."

"Tell me about that," Allie asked.

"Every afternoon for about an hour, the most beautiful singing is heard all over the city. Those who have listened claim the voices are as clear as the most perfect glass. They are as pure as the most perfect chime. People suggested it was the Loving Couple's voices, that the Gods themselves were singing to their creation. We know the Gods love people who live in the country as much as they do the people in the city. So, we wondered why we couldn't hear them. Why would they not sing to us too?"

"Do you know anything else about this singing?" Allie asked.

The man shook his head. "Only what I told you," he answered. "It happens for about an hour every afternoon. The singing is beautiful, beyond description. We don't hear it in the country. That is all we know."

"Tell me more about the Triumvirate," Allie asked.

"Wonderful people," the first man said immediately. "Two sisters and a brother. Triplets. The most handsome people you could imagine. Congrata, Exeta, and their brother Lexitus. They are so distinguished and gifted. They are as smart as they are beautiful. They have served the city in so many ways. Everyone supported them for Consul and they won the election in a landslide. Like I said, we don't get as much news here in the country, but everyone in the city seemed happy with them and wished them success.

"I don't know what they are doing to combat this curse that has gripped the city," the man continued. "I pray they are not in a trance like all the others. If they are, we have no hope. That is why we have come to the temple. We pray every minute that this curse will end."

"Do you mind if we visit with the other pilgrims and spend time with them?" Allie asked the men.

"Everyone is welcome at the Temple of the Loving Couple," the second man answered graciously. "Please be our guests. Join us. We have food. We have shelter. Pray with us if you wish."

The girls wandered away from the two men. The two crews felt safe, still the cloaked boys followed closely. The men were so friendly; they didn't worry about trouble with the other pilgrims. Eventually, the girls sat under a tree. The boys sat next to them and uncloaked.

"We have answered one of history's biggest mysteries," Mike announced. Everyone looked at him questioningly. All they had learned was the city's name, Alayniess. None of them had ever heard of this place. What had been solved? Mike observed their expressions and realized they didn't understand. He explained, "The way words are pronounced changes over time. That's what happened with the name Alayniess. We say it differently, but it's easy to see how the changes happened. Listen closely. Al-ay-ni-ess became At-layn-tess. That became At-lan-tis. Get it? We have discovered the lost city of Atlantis."

The questioning expression on the time crews' faces changed to stunned surprise. They couldn't believe their find. Had they really stumbled upon the legendary Atlantis? Scholars had always said Atlantis was a myth because there was no proof it ever existed. The ancient Greeks told stories about Atlantis, but there was no evidence. The reason became clear to the crews. According to the Greek legend, Atlantis existed only a short time before their own civilization. That was wrong. The city had disappeared 10,000 years before the ancient Greeks, while modern humans were still living in caves.

After a long period of silence, Nick announced to the others, "I know what's causing the trance. And I think I can stop it."

"Okay, Inspector Gadget," Patrick said. "What have you figured out that the rest of us are missing?"

"It's the music," Nick replied, like the answer was so obvious everyone should get it. "It has to be the music that's causing the trance. It's the only constant. The crews at the dig heard the music. They went into a trance. Allie, you heard the music at the dig and you went into a trance. People here get a dose of the music every afternoon, and they go into a trance. It has to be the music."

"Do you think what happened to me is the same as happened to those people in the city?" Allie asked. "Why did it take me three days and them only two?"

"I don't have all the answers," Nick replied, shrugging his shoulders. "You said the music you heard in the dig was faint. Maybe it took longer to overcome you because you didn't hear it as well. You said you thought the music could be voices singing, rather than instruments. The men just told us; there is no doubt it is singing. The questions now are: Who is doing it? How are they doing it? Why?"

"You said you could stop the trance?" Patrick asked. "How?"

"Let me take care of that," Nick replied. "Lenore, let's go back to the craft. I need your help." Nick and Lenore left the group while the rest sat under the tree and talked about what they had learned. After several hours they wandered back to the craft. Inside they found Nick and Lenore wearing their helmets. They were taking turns singing silly songs to each other, and giggling.

"You guys came back here for this?" Patrick asked in surprise. "I thought you had some big idea."

"We did," Nick answered, still giggling. "And I think it will work. Here, put on this helmet." When Patrick was ready Nick sang, "Mary had a little lamb. Its fleece was white as snow." He asked Patrick, "Did you hear that?" Patrick nodded. "Did you notice anything?" Nick asked the pilot.

"Yeah," Patrick answered. "Your voice sounded different and every note was sour. It's a good thing Mike is our singer."

"Right," Nick said with a smile. "You heard me in a different pitch and off key. The man told us how beautiful and perfect the singing is. I'm guessing that may be how it hypnotizes people. I'm hoping I can take away its power by making it off key. The helmet will change the pitch before you hear it. The music will sound like a bunch of sour notes."

"Good thinking," Mike said. "How did you do it?"

"Uh…." Nick hesitated.

"Oh no!" Mike yelled. "You took my Pitch Perfect. Blast it, Nick. How many times do I have to tell you to leave my stuff alone? I never even got to try the thing out."

"Settle down, Egghead," Patrick said to Mike. "Tell me Nick, is the person wearing this helmet the only one protected?"

"Lenore and I need to work on your helmets," Nick told the others. "This helmet changes the pitch, and then it sends the sound to all the others. If my idea works for my helmet, it should work for all yours. We should all be protected."

"Get to work," Patrick told his engineer. "I suggest we go into the city tomorrow afternoon and test these things."

Meanwhile, Mike was so frustrated he sat on the bench with his head in his hands.

CHAPTER TEN
THE WEEPING MAN

The two time craft – bundled into one - landed in the city. They placed themselves at the edge of the plaza below the domed building. "How do you plan to test the helmets?" Patrick asked Nick.

"I don't know," Nick answered. "Anyone have any ideas?"

Mike lifted his head out of his hands. The annoyance at losing his Pitch Perfect still showed on his face. "Yeah," he said in answer to his pilot's question. "When scientists want to test something they give it to a guinea pig to see what happens. We need a guinea pig. Two people have to go outside to listen to the singing. One will wear Nick's helmet and be protected. The other will be wearing a regular helmet. If the unprotected person goes into a trance and the protected one doesn't, you will know the helmets work. The one wearing Nick's helmet will be there to bring the hypnotized guinea pig back to safety. There's no danger. We know people recover in a couple of days."

"What if the helmets don't work and both people go into a trance?" Jen asked.

"Easy," Mike replied. "While they're outside, they have to stay close to the craft. If both are hypnotized, we run out and rescue them."

No one could find a flaw with the plan. "Who's the guinea pig?" Lenore asked.

"I am," Mike responded firmly. "I'm an S/O. Knowledge is my line of work." He was still embarrassed at having missed the wavy hair and brown eyes shared by all Atlanteans. This would make up a bit for his goof.

"What about Allie?" Jen asked. "She's an S/O too."

"That's right," Mike agreed. "But Allie has already been in a trance. If I go under this time, two of us will have had the experience. We increase our knowledge." Allie nodded her head in agreement and squeezed Mike's handing lovingly. "The sun is directly overhead," Mike told the friends. "That means it's about noon. Nick and I may have to wait several hours. We only know the singing starts in the afternoon. We don't know exactly when."

Mike and Nick put on their helmets. They didn't bother to cloak. It was safe outside. Except for the people who were working, everyone in the plaza was standing like statues, staring straight ahead. The two friends sat in a shady spot on a sidewalk close to the craft. The crew inside could see them easily and could rescue them in seconds if anything went wrong.

Nothing did. Mike and Nick passed the time talking. They studied the buildings around the plaza and watched the construction. They napped. After several hours of doing nothing, Mike and Nick suddenly looked up. The crews knew from their reaction that the music had started. The two time travelers on the sidewalk listened carefully. Then, they looked around the plaza to find where the music was coming from. They checked out the people in the distance. It was obvious to their friends that Nick and Mike were observing, trying to learn everything they could. Allie asked Jen to open the door. She reached outside and placed a recording device on the ground. "I want to record the singing so researchers at UNH can analyze it," she explained.

About an hour later, the S/O and engineer returned to the craft. Those watching them knew the music had ended. Inside, Nick and Mike took off their helmets. "How do you feel?" Allie asked them.

"I'm fine," Nick replied. "Listening to someone sing off key for an hour was torture, but I'm fine."

"I'm lightheaded," Mike said. "It's kinda how you feel if you wake up suddenly from a deep sleep with lots of dreams. You know, it takes a while to adjust. But I feel good."

"I hate to do this to you guys," Jen said. "Until we know more, I think we all need to stay in the craft where it's safe." Patrick nodded.

"Don't do that to us again," Nick begged. "It is so crowded in here. Until tomorrow, take us out of the city into the country. I can't stay cooped up in this craft one more day." Jen and Patrick looked at each other and nodded in agreement. It was unfair to keep someone as tall as Nick cramped in a small time craft cabin with five other people and a dog.

The next afternoon, the craft returned to the same spot as the previous day. Mike and Nick exited and sat on their sidewalk again. Just like yesterday, they waited while their friends in the Auckland watched. The time travelers in the craft knew again when the music started. Mike and Nick stood and looked around. Once again, they were trying to discover anything they could about this strange sound, especially its source. After a while, Nick was the only one looking about. Mike had his back to the craft and seemed to be examining a wall. This went on for a moment before Allie realized what had happened. "He's in the trance," she announced.

Jen opened the door and called to Nick, "Nick, it's happened. Mike's in a trance." Nick looked at his friend's face and nodded back to the craft. Yup. Mike was gone. The engineer took the S/O by the arm and told him to walk back to the craft. Mike obeyed without any reaction. He just stared straight ahead.

Jen opened the door again so the two Fixers could enter the craft. Nick told Mike to sit. He did, still staring. "Well, that settles it," Patrick announced. "We've proven two things. The music causes the trance, and the helmets work. We know it will take a couple of days for

Mike to snap out of it. Why don't we return to the country and wait. Nick, you and Lenore can wire the other helmets while we're there."

Back where they had spent the previous night, Allie led Mike out of the craft and sat him on the grass. The others spread out to enjoy the warm tropical afternoon. After a long period of silence while everyone enjoyed the day, Patrick whispered, "Hey, Nick. You want to try an experiment?" Nick nodded. He was bored and was interested in whatever the pilot had in mind. "Good," Patrick said with a devilish look in his eye. "Mike," he called to his S/O. "You are a chicken. Act like one." Still staring straight ahead, Mike stood and put his hands to his armpits, and flapped his elbows like they were wings. He scratched at the ground with his feet. "Crow like a rooster," Patrick laughed. Mike did his best rooster imitation.

"Stop that," Jen yelled. "Patrick Weaver, you should be ashamed of yourself! You are humiliating your friend." Patrick tried to act serious while Jen scolded him. It was impossible. Behind Jen, Patrick could see Nick rolling on the ground in laughter. Nick's laughing was infectious and set off the pilot. Patrick's face turned red, and when he could hold out no longer, he burst into uncontrollable giggles. Jen stamped her foot and turned to Lenore and Allie for support. Her two friends were trying to be serious, but the grins on their faces revealed that they were about to break out laughing as well. Meanwhile, Mike went about flapping, scratching, and crowing.

After two days of waiting, Mike came out of the trance. It was a long slow process. He said afterward it reminded him of the time he had his tonsils removed. Waking up after the operation seemed to take forever, as he drifted between being asleep and being awake. He would open his eyes and talk to his parents and then pass out again. He remembered nothing about the operation and only had dim memories of the drifting. Going into the trance was the same. Mike said he remembered being lightheaded and feeling like he was floating. Next, he found himself on the grass outside the city. Like being under anesthesia, Mike couldn't remember anything that happened while he was in the trance.

The two pilots landed their craft at the edge of the plaza and the crews exited, each person wearing a translator helmet. All the helmets had been wired to make the singing sound off key. The singing would have no power over these six people. Allie had Menlo on his leash. The time travelers didn't bother to cloak. No one in the plaza paid any attention to them.

The group walked through the plaza, watching the construction. The hypnotized workers were moving yet another jig saw block into place, and the statues had more detail than they did several days earlier.

Otherwise, the place was the same as when Mike went into his trance.

Everything was the same except for one small item. Mike was the first to notice and pointed it out to his friends. A man was sitting on the wide steps that led from the plaza up to the domed building. He had his face in his hands and he was shaking. "That guy isn't acting like he's in a trance," Mike said. "Let's try talking to him. Remember, the less he knows about us the better. Tell him as little as possible."

The time travelers and their dog climbed the steps to the man, Mike in the lead. The man was so absorbed by his grief the crews got very close before he realized they were there. He looked up in surprise at the approaching strangers. Mike looked at him in equal surprise. "Dr. Newcomb!" he blurted. "What are you doing here?"

The man stared in stunned silence as the other strangers came up behind the first. They all asked the same thing. "Dr. Newcomb. What are you doing here?"

"Who are you?" the man stammered. "You men are tall. You must be from the tribes across the ocean to the east. Why are you not wearing skins?" He looked at Nick with amazement and a bit of fear. The long, thin time traveler was a foot taller than he.

"What is that creature?" the man asked, pointing at Menlo. "I have heard that the tall cave people have animals that live with them. When anything approaches the cave those creatures make a frightening sound."

"Dr. Newcomb. Don't you know us?' Mike asked. He wondered if his teacher and friend had been in a trance. Perhaps he was just coming out of it and was still confused.

"Dr. Newcomb. What does this mean?" the man replied.

"That is your name," Allie answered. "It is what everyone at the Institute calls you."

"My name is Carolus Nukium," the man insisted. "I do not know this Dr. Newcomb."

The time crews studied the man's face closely. In spite of a being almost a perfect twin, the man was not lying. He was not Dr. Newcomb. His hair had not turned as gray as Dr. Newcomb's, and his face did not have as many wrinkles. This man was probably ten years younger than the man in the distant future he so closely resembled.

"We apologize for our mistake," Mike said. "It's just that you look so much like our friend. We mistook you for him. We're sorry if we startled you."

"I am fine," the man said. The crews knew this was false. The man's eyes were red from crying. "Who are you?" he asked again. "Where do you come from?"

"We're explorers," Allie answered. It worked last time. She hoped it would work again. Remembering Mike's advice, she changed the subject. "We noticed you were crying," she said. "You look so much like our friend; we can't help but be concerned. Can we help you? Can you tell us what is the matter?"

Carolus examined the faces in front of him and saw expressions of true concern for his feelings. He pointed out at the plaza and to the sprawling city beyond. "This is the Eternal City," he began. "It is blessed by the Loving Couple who have always provided for us. They gave us our republic. With their guidance and blessing, we have always governed ourselves as a free people. We have always lived in peace and liberty."

"They don't look like free people," Lenore observed, glancing at the Atlanteans in the plaza.

"They are slaves," Carolus said in disgust.

"What causes the trance?" Mike asked.

"I don't know," Carolus answered. "One day, everyone in the city heard singing. It was so beautiful we thought it was the Loving Couple, singing in joy to their people. The next day, this happened." He stretched out his hand and pointed at the robot-like people in the plaza. "The singing happens every afternoon, but if it is the Loving Couple, they are wasting their time. Their people have become slaves of the Triumvirate."

The time travelers were amazed that Carolus had not connected the singing to the trance. "What do you think causes the trance?" Nick asked.

"I do not know," Carolus answered. "Perhaps the Triumvirate is causing it, perhaps not. I do know they are using it to their advantage. They are using these hypnotized people as slaves to build memorials to themselves. Do you see those three statues being carved?" The time travelers nodded. The last time they were in the plaza they had watched work being done on them. "Those statues are images of Congrata, Exeta, and their brother Lexitus. They are the only statues in all of Alayniess honoring people. We have statues of the Gods and of mythical beings. We Alaynians have always been honored to serve the city, and we have never honored ourselves for our service."

"If those statues are what the Triumvirate really looks like, they are handsome people," Lenore observed.

"They are," Carolus responded. "They were handsome even as babies. As adults, they are beautiful. As children, it was obvious to everyone that they had great abilities and great promise. We encouraged them. We gave them the best education. We trained them in many skills. When they came of age, we gave them positions of responsibility. The last election they ran for the Consulate and won. They are our consuls. Congrata has been First Consul for two years."

"How does the Consulate work," Mike asked?

"Our government has three branches. Our legislature makes the laws. Our courts ensure everyone is treated equally. The third is the Consulate. We elect three consuls to run the government. They serve six years. The First Consul is the leader for two years. The other two are advisors. The next two years, one of the other consuls is First Consul. The third consul is First Consul for the last two years. Then, we elect three more people for the next six years."

"How is the Triumvirate taking advantage of the singing?" Nick asked.

"They are using people to build monuments," Carolus replied. "They make no effort to stop the music, or to protect the people from it. They use them as slaves. They tell me they are building an Empire that will be more glorious than the Republic."

"That raises an important question," Mike observed. "How come you can talk to the Triumvirate? How come everyone else is in a trance except you and them?"

"I don't know," Carolus said, hanging his head. "I don't know. I wish I was in a trance. Then, I would not know my beloved city was enslaved and our republic being destroyed. I know I am different from all the other people, but I don't know why. I don't know why the sisters and their brother are also different."

"You call this the Eternal City," Jen said. "Why? Tell us your history."

"Alayniess is eternal because it has always been here. We realize that our very distant ancestors must have built the city, but we don't know when, it was so long ago. Our histories go back tens of thousands of years. Even those earliest histories speak of Alayniess as an old city."

"Tell us about those rods," Nick said. "What are they? How do they work?"

"We Alaynians are proud of our art and our literature. They make our lives very pleasant. However, our greatest accomplishments are our mathematics and our science. The Loving Couple placed the sun in the sky. They placed this land on the middle of the earth where the sun is always bright. They placed us here on this land and taught us to make use of the sun. The sun provides us with all our power. That power brings the granite here from around the world. It moves the blocks into place. It carves the granite. It does all our work for us. I am a writer, not a scientist. So, I cannot explain how things work, other than to say we use power from the sun."

Carolus continued. "I can tell you a story of how great our science is; how it saved us from disaster. Many hundreds of years ago, the great blankets of ice to the north began to melt, and all that new water caused the seas to rise. Our land began to flood. We would have been lost beneath the waves but for our science. Using the sun's power, our scientists cut our land loose from the earth below. Today, that same power holds our land on the surface of the ocean so we do not sink. Unlike other lands on this earth, Alayniess floats."

"That is amazing!" Nick and Lenore said together. "I would love to talk to some scientists," Nick added. "This technology is unlike anything we have. It is a completely different idea from our technology."

"I am afraid our scientists can't talk any longer," Carolus said sadly. He stretched his arm toward the plaza below. "They are all in a trance like these people."

"What will you do?" Allie asked. "Will you remain here and try to save your people?"

"It is no use," Carolus answered, tears welling again in his eyes. "I have tried to change the Triumvirate's mind. It is no use. I have a plan for myself. I will do what the Triumvirate has told me. Soon, I will go across the sea to the lands to the east. There, I will find some of the tall people living in caves; the ones who hunt meat with sharp stones on the ends of sticks. I will live with them. I will learn to be like them. I won't go to the short ones. There are not many of them anymore. I don't think they have a future.

"Among the tall people I will find a woman and marry. I will pass on to my sons whatever it is about me that makes me different from other Alaynians. My sons will be different too. I will tell my sons to tell their sons, to tell their sons: in every Nukium generation name a boy Carolus. That way, even when I am long-forgotten, my family will know who has inherited my difference, who can listen to the music without going into a trance, who can save Alayniess. That will be my mark. I will pass it on forever, until someone from among my descendants rescues my people."

"How will you get to the lands to the east," Lenore asked.

"I have a boat ready in the canal," Carolus said. "I will sail down the canal to the sea. Then, I will sail to the east. I will never see my beloved city again. But someday, because of my plan, my children's children may save it." He began to sob violently and put his face in his hands.

As the time travelers stared at the weeping man the afternoon singing began. "Wow," Mike said commenting on the sound he heard through his helmet. "That really is sour and off key. It hurts my ears."

"I would like to know where the Triumvirate is and what they are doing right now," Nick said.

"They are in there," Carolus answered, lifting his head. His face was red from crying. His cheeks were soaked by the tears that ran down to his chin. He waved his hand at the domed building behind him. "They come out through that door. The one surrounded by guards."

Patrick waved to his friends to follow him as he began to climb the steps to the building. "Wait guys," Mike said when the group was far enough away from Carolus to talk. "I've figured some things out." The others gathered around him to listen. "Carolus said his people have been here for tens of thousands of years, and the city was old even then. Do you realize what the Alaynians are? They're another species of humans. They're not exactly the same as us. They have some different genes. That's why they all have wavy brown hair and brown eyes. To top it off, they're a very advanced species. Look at their technology. Our ancestors are still living in caves.

"Their ancestors must have wandered here from Africa tens of thousands of years ago. When the ocean levels were low because of the glacier, they could have walked here on dry ground. When the seas began to rise, Atlantis became an island. Their evolution followed its own path, separate from the other human species.

Guys, we have discovered an unknown type of human. It's not just modern humans and Neanderthals living on the earth right now. There are also Atlanteans. This is a major discovery for anthropologists!

"Second thing," Mike continued. "Remember Dr. MacDonald's talk to our class about genes and mutations? Carolus has a mutation. That's why he can listen to the music and not go into a trance. He's right. He will pass that mutation on to his children. However, they will not save the city. We know that soon, in less than several lifetimes, it disappears. Remember how many times we flew over this spot and only saw ocean? This place is doomed. Atlantis has no future, and the Triumvirate will not enjoy its empire for long."

"I agree with Nick," Patrick said. "We need to find that Triumvirate. I think we've all reached the same conclusion. They are involved in this."

"How are we going to get through that line of guards?" Mike asked. "They have their arms linked and their legs crossed. We couldn't sneak through even if we cloaked."

"I'm going to tell them to act like chickens," Patrick answered. Mike's surprised expression showed that he did not understand, and certainly didn't remember. "Never mind," Patrick answered. "It's an old joke between Nick and me." Sure enough, Patrick walked up to the line of men with linked arms. "Listen to me," he announced. "I'm sure the Triumvirate told you not to listen to Carolus Nukium. I am not Carolus Nukium. So, do as I tell you. You are all chickens. Act like chickens!"

The orderly line of men turned into a crazy barnyard scene as they strutted around clucking and crowing and flapping their wings. Their heads bobbed up and down. "Let's go," Patrick told his friends. The time travelers laughed out loud as they walked by the imitation chickens.

Inside the building, Jen advised, "We're out of sight. Carolus can't see us any longer. We should cloak. We don't know what we're going to find, but it will be safer if no one can see us." Everyone put on their night vision goggles and their head covers and gloves. Allie pulled Menlo's cover over his head. Each time traveler touched a switch on his or her chest and disappeared. Jen pushed the button on her remote and Menlo was no longer there either. Anyone walking by would think the hall was as empty as it had been before the crews entered.

The time travelers passed several offices. Books and documents were scattered on desks. Patrick signaled the others to wait while he checked out an office. He remembered that Chaz was looking for writing and took some papers from a desk. He folded them and put them in his pocket. His friends waiting in the hall knew what he had done, and why.

The group passed several more rooms before the six found what they were seeking. In a windowless chamber they spotted the Triumvirate. Everyone's first reaction was the same. These three people were beautiful! The girls admired Lexitus and gave him a long examination. The boys couldn't take their eyes off

Congrata and Exeta. A long moment later, the group regained its senses and focused on what the Triumvirate was doing. They were standing around a tube that rose out of the floor. And, they were singing.

"There's our answer," Mike whispered to his friends. "I don't know how they do it, but I'd like to learn their trick. If The Sirens could sing like that, all our albums would go platinum. All we would have to do is tell everyone to buy a copy. They'd be in a trance and obey. We'd be rich."

Allie reached into her pocket and took out her recorder. "I want to record them live, as well," she explained.

The teams watched and listened to the Triumvirate until they had finished singing. Then, the three consuls turned and entered a granite chamber at the back of the room. The chamber was small, more like a vault. They began to work on the vault. The teams did not understand Atlantean science, so they had no idea what the three were doing.

Mike Dunbar

CHAPTER ELEVEN
SABOTAGE

Just before leaving the building the teams uncloaked. They were still inside the door and out of sight of Carolus Nukium, so he didn't see them suddenly appear. Outside, they found their flock of chickens still crowing, clucking, and flapping. Carolus still stood on his step below the building and stared at the guards' antics. His mouth hung open in disbelief. The two crews walked past the guards. When they reached the top step Patrick turned. "All done," he said to his chickens in a command voice. "Go back to your guard positions." The men lined up. They again linked arms and crossed legs like nothing had happened.

The crews sat on the step with Carolus. "Going into that building was worthwhile," Patrick began. "We know lots more than we did before. We saw the Triumvirate. We watched them singing." He passed his hand in the direction of the plaza and the hypnotized workers. "They are the cause of all this. Did you know they could sing?"

"No," Carolus answered in awe and shock. "But they have many talents."

"They were singing into a tube," Jen added. "Do you know about this tube? Do you know what it is, or where it goes?"

Carolus shook his head. "No, but they are the Consuls. They are responsible for all public works. They have the authority to build the tube, whatever it is."

"I bet they have known for a long time that they have this ability to hypnotize people by singing," Allie said. "I bet they have been planning this power grab for years. That's why they got themselves elected to the Consulate. In office, they would have authority. They could build whatever they needed to carry out their plan. The question remains, what is that tube?"

"If one end of the tube is in their chamber and the singing is heard outside, it's a pretty safe bet the tube comes out of the building," Nick said. "If we could locate it out here, maybe we could mess up their plan."

"I'm sure they wouldn't leave the tube out in the open," Lenore added. "They would have hidden it."

"We have a companion who is real good at finding things," Mike said, pointing at Menlo. The dog saw the gesture and perked up. He realized Mike had something in mind, and he was ready to do whatever his master asked of him. "The next time the singing begins," Mike added. "I'll have Menlo look for the place where the tube comes out of the building."

"That means we have another day to kill," Patrick observed. Turning to the Atlantean he asked, "Carolus, can you meet us here tomorrow afternoon at the same time?" Carolus agreed. The teams noticed that the man was less troubled, like he had found a ray of hope. He knew what was causing the trance, and there was a chance his new friends could stop it. If so, Atlantis could go back to the way it had always been.

The next afternoon the time travelers and the Atlantean met again on the steps that led up from the plaza to the domed building. Only one thing was different from the day before. Nick carried a bag on his shoulder. He had brought tools with him. Not long after the group reunited with Carolus, the singing began again. Mike took Menlo by the leash. "Nick, Carolus, come along and help me," he said. The three climbed to the top of the steps. On the upper platform, Menlo stopped and looked at the row of hypnotized guards with linked arms. He didn't like the look of them and gave a low growl. "It's okay, Mennie," Mike said, reassuring the dog that the men were harmless. He bent over and let the dog off his leash. Then he said, "Menlo, find it."

The dog started off at a trot with his nose to the ground. As he traveled he turned to the right and then to the left. He repeated that over and over, so he moved ahead in a wavy pattern. "Menlo doesn't know what he's looking for, but he'll tell us when he finds something," Mike explained to Nick. "It's is a trick Kwasi taught him when we were lost in Nowhere."

Carolus didn't know who Kwasi was, or about Nowhere, and he didn't ask any questions. He was too interested in watching Menlo hunt. He had never seen a dog before. "I understand why the tall people to the east keep these creatures," he said. "If you live by hunting animals for food, they are very helpful."

Menlo worked his way along the side of the building, continually turning left and then right. He stopped several times and listened. Other times, he put his nose in the air and sniffed. Finally, he stopped and scratched at a spot on the ground. When the dog's companions caught up with him, Nick examined the place that interested Menlo. It was a granite stone in the sidewalk that looked just like all the others. Nick dropped his bag on the ground. He got on his hands and knees and examined the stone closely. He knocked on the granite with his knuckles. "It's not a block of stone," he said. "It's a panel made to look like stone."

Nick reached into his bag and pulled out a tool similar to a screw driver. He pried at the edges of the panel until it came loose. He lifted the panel and found himself looking into a tunnel. Still on his knees, Nick stuck his head into the hole to examine the space. "It's part of the city's drainage system," he said. His voiced echoed inside the hole. "There are drain pipes in there, but I can see the tube too."

Nick stood up and described what he had seen to Carolus and Mike. "It looks like they ran the tube through the city's drainage tunnels. It's clever. No one would have been suspicious. When they built the tube, it would have appeared that normal repair work was being done." Nick looked at the opening, judging its size. "I'm skinny enough to fit in there," he said. "Carolus, you're small. You'll fit too. Mike, you won't. Stay here with Menlo. Carolus and I will do some more exploring."

Mike watched his friend and the Atlantean crawl into the opening. It was tight, but they made it. He saw their feet slowly disappear into the dark, leaving him alone with his dog. Half an hour had passed when Mike heard noises coming from the tunnel. He knew his two companions were returning. Nick crawled out first. While Carolus wiggled out of the opening Nick told Mike what he had done. "The tube is a broadcasting system. It is very clever. The sound travels down the tube and hits things that look like drum heads. The sound bounces off the drum heads and is amplified, made louder. Then, it is sent down other tubes to more drum heads. It goes all over the city that way. That's why people in the country don't hear the singing. The drainage system is only under the city. Those three people inside that building are real smart."

"Can we stop the singing from being broadcast around the city?" Mike asked.

"It's already done," Nick replied. "I cut the pipe into pieces. Then, I put the pieces together so they made a great big loop. I secured the pieces together with duct tape. As the Triumvirate sings, the sound travels around the loop and goes back to them. They will hear their own echo. The sound doesn't go anywhere else, just back to them. We need to return to the others," Nick advised. "As soon as the Triumvirate realizes something's wrong, I think we're gonna hear from them."

The three joined their friends back on the steps. Nick had just enough time to warn the others to be prepared when a flurry of activity broke out at the domed building's doorway. Sure enough, it was the Triumvirate marching out. Patrick whispered to the others, "Get behind Carolus and cloak." The time travelers stepped back and disappeared. Carolus didn't notice. To the Triumvirate, it looked like their enemy was standing on the steps all by himself.

There was no doubt from the expressions on the Triumvirate's faces, they were angry. "What have you done, Carolus?" Congrata demanded. The triplets stood safely behind their line of guards. "You have sabotaged us."

"I know what you have been doing," Carolus laughed, "and I have stopped you. You can sing all you want. The people of Alayniess can no longer hear you. Soon, they will come out of their trance. When they do, they will not be happy with the Triumvirate. Your days in power will be over. You will be disgraced and punished."

"It was a mistake to let you live, Carolus," Lexitus spat in anger. "I wish I had gotten a stick with a sharp stone from those primitives to the east. I would have stabbed you like they stab animals to kill them. Then, you would never have become a bother. If I ever have the chance, that is what I will do to you. I will kill you! I swear to you, Carolus. I will kill you."

"Too late," Carolus laughed. "You're not going to kill anyone."

"Don't be so sure," Exeta replied bitterly to her enemy standing below her on the stairs. "Yes, it is too late. It is too late for you, Carolus. It is too late for Alayniess. Do you think we are unprepared? Surely you don't think we are without another plan, in case this one went wrong. Surely you don't think we would allow the people to punish us. We are the best Alayniess has ever produced. We will not be punished by people who are inferior to us. Remember this as you watch the disaster happen. It is your fault. Alayniess could have chosen our Empire. The catastrophe is your fault."

"You have not defeated us, Carolus," Congrata added. "You have only delayed us. You are finished, but we are not. We will be back. We and our Empire will rise again, and we will bring the glory of Alayniess back with us. We will restore to her a greater glory than she has ever known." With that, the Triumvirate marched back into the domed building and closed the door behind them.

The time teams uncloaked before Carolus was able to turn around. He did not realize they had been invisible all the time he was talking with the Triumvirate. "What do you think they meant?" Carolus asked the crews. "They talked about a catastrophe, about a disaster. They talked about coming back. Do you think they were talking about the end of their empire? When my people come out of the trance those three will be removed as consuls. Do they hope to take power again? Are they so foolish as to think Alayniess would elect them a second time? They are finished. We are done with them. They will be fortunate if they are not banished to the country."

"I don't know what they meant," Jen answered. "But I didn't like the sound of it. I think we'd better get back inside that building and see what those three are up to.

"I didn't like what I heard either," Patrick agreed. "Follow me," he told the others as he ran up the stairs. "Carolus, come with us.

"Sorry, guys," Patrick said as he charged the line of men with their arms linked. "No time to play chicken." At a full run, Patrick's strong, short body slammed into the smaller, hypnotized guards. It was like a bowling ball hitting ten pins. Five of the men were lifted off their feet and fell on their backs. Those standing next to them were dragged down. "Carolus, get in there!" Patrick commanded at a yell, directing his companions through the hole he had created. "The rest of you; Go! Go! Go!"

One after another Carolus and the time travelers charged through the hole in the line. They entered the building and ran down the hallway, arriving at the chamber where the Triumvirate did their singing. They were just in time to see three pairs of legs disappear into the granite vault at the back of the chamber. They could only see legs because a massive granite door was slowly lowering and sealing the opening.

The crews and Carolus slammed their shoulders against the thick granite door as it settled into position. It was useless. The heavy stone door was not going to be raised by mere flesh and blood. It would require a crane, or some of the rods being used in the plaza. "The rods," Nick cried as he realized what he needed. "We have to get some of those rods. They will raise that door."

The group ran back down the hall and out of the building. After being scattered by Patrick the line of men had reformed. Once again, they were standing at attention with their arms linked and their legs crossed. This time, Patrick smashed through them from behind, bowling the men head over heels.

As the time travelers and the Atlantean reached the top step, the group heard a deafening BOOM. The noise was so loud and powerful their chests quivered from the vibration. They saw the whole city shudder. Carolus stopped and called to the time crew who were just about to descend the stairs to the plaza, "Wait. What is going on?" Next, the group felt the ground beneath their feet quiver, like they were standing on gelatin.

"Oh no!" Carolus yelled in horror. He realized what was happening. "Oh no! This can't be! They are so evil! How could they do this? Oh Alayniess, Alayniess...."

"What is it?" Mike demanded.

"They have cut off the power that keeps Alayniess afloat," Carolus cried with terror in his eyes. "The city is sinking!"

"That's what they meant," Lenore replied. "Remember they said they would rise again? They would sink first. What did they mean when they said they would bring Atlantis back and restore her to a greater glory? How can they do that if everyone is dead?"

"How long will it take for the city to sink," Jen asked Carolus.

"Not long," the frantic Atlantean replied. "Not long. I have to think. What do I do?"

"You do what you planned," Mike answered. "You get to the canal. You get in your boat and you sail away from here. Get to the people in the east and live with them. Pass on to your sons what makes you different. Name a son Carolus and teach every generation to do the same. Get going. If you stay here, you die with the city."

Carolus stared at Mike for a long moment. He was stunned and needed to collect his thoughts. "Yes, yes," he finally agreed with confusion in his voice. "Of course, that's what I have to do." The Atlantean left the time travelers and charged down the stairs. The last time the crews saw Carolus Nukium, he was running across the plaza towards the canal.

"We have to get out of here too," Jen said with fear in her voice. "Run for the craft." The crews and Menlo set off at a run down the stairs and across the plaza. Once inside the Auckland's cabin, Jen and Patrick lifted the two time craft into the air. Hovering above the city they could safely watch the catastrophe occur. A low wall of water flowed in from all sides. The ocean was claiming Atlantis as its own. High in the air, the crews were horrified as they thought about what was happening to the people below. The pilgrims they had met at the temple were closest to the coast. They were already gone. Allie and Lenore remembered the two men who had been so friendly with them.

It comforted the time travelers to realize that the people in the city were in a trance, and unaware of what was happening. They were not fearful or panicked. They went down peacefully, still staring straight ahead.

The crews continued to watch as the city sank deeper and deeper. In the far future, the domed building was first to rise out of the sea. Now, it was the last thing remaining above the surface of the waves. Slowly, it too disappeared. As it sank out of sight, the sea turned into a gigantic whirlpool. A half hour later, the waters stopped swirling and monstrous waves swept together from every direction. The waves ran into each other with such force the sea became a carpet of white foam. After an hour the sea had settled and assumed its normal appearance. Thousands of everyday objects floated on the surface. They were all that was left of Atlantis.

The crews waited to see if there were any survivors. There were not. Little by little, the floating objects either sank or drifted away. Eventually, there was no sign that Atlantis had ever existed. The ocean was empty, just like it would be in the future, every time the crews had flown over it while looking for the city.

Atlantis was gone. It had been brought to an end by its own children. Atlanteans had loved the gifted triplets. When they were young, they had been given the best education. They had been taught many skills. Finally, they had been given the authority to govern the city, but they had used that authority to turn their people into slaves. Now, rather than surrender to their people, they had destroyed their city and everyone in it.

The two time craft continued to circle the empty spot in the ocean. Looking out a porthole window Nick noticed a white object on the horizon. "What's that?" he asked.

Mike squinted. "It's a sail," he answered. "It's a boat sailing away. I think I know who's in the boat. It looks like Carolus escaped. He's on his way to find those cavemen. I wish him luck."

"Oh, my word!" Allie suddenly exclaimed. "Jen, Patrick. Get us back to Chaz as fast as you can." Mike looked at her with concern, and a bit of jealousy. Why all of a sudden did Allie want to see Chaz? "Don't you get it?" she asked the others as they stared at her with surprise. "I heard singing at the dig and went into a trance. We didn't know what the music was then, but we do now. It was the Triumvirate. They said they would rise again. That's what's happening at the dig. They're coming back. Those people are in danger. We have to get there immediately."

As the two craft returned to their own time, Lenore looked worried. "Did we make a mistake?" she asked. "Did we change time? Have we set off Chaos?"

Mike and Allie pondered those questions. "We know the city had disappeared below the waves before we got there," Mike said. "While we were looking for the city we flew over open sea numerous times. It wasn't there. We weren't responsible for the catastrophe. I don't know what to think about Carolus' escape. Did he follow his original sequence?"

"He had already planned to leave Atlantis," Allie replied. "He had his boat ready at the canal. We saw his sail, but we don't know if he ever made it to land. We don't know if he found the modern humans. We don't know if he married, or if he had sons. Whatever he did, he was going to do it anyway. He followed his sequence. I don't think we changed anything." The rest of the crews nodded in relief. They had not violated Time Institute ethics.

CHAPTER TWELVE
THE RETURN

Jen and Patrick landed their craft near the dig and Jen opened the Auckland's door. The crews were surprised by what they saw. The scene was very much like another one they had recently witnessed, the one when they had met Carolus Nukium. In this case it was Chaz. He sat in a chair at the campsite with his head in his hands. The archaeologists and geologists he had brought with him were guarding the transports. Their arms were linked just like the guards who had stood in front of the domed building. These people too stared straight ahead.

"Didn't we return to our frame of origination?" Mike asked. "When did all this happen?" he said, surprised at how much had changed since they had left on their mission.

"Don't you remember," Jen reminded him. "After we left, we spent several days camping on that hillside in Spain. That's when all this took place. While we were enjoying a couple of days off, the Triumvirate returned. It looks like they have come and gone. Notice that one of the transports is missing. They must have taken it."

"Yeah," Mike replied, a little embarrassed again. One of the pilots had spotted an important detail that he, a trained S/O, had missed. He consoled himself by recalling that pilots pay attention to craft. Of course, Jen would notice if one was missing. In a while he would have picked up on that detail too.

Menlo was off his leash and trotted alongside Allie. When he noticed the people with their locked arms, he stopped and came to attention. His J-shaped tail stood up over his back. He relaxed when he realized he had seen a line of people standing like this before. The others had not been a threat, so he decided these people weren't either. Next, Menlo spotted Chaz sitting with his face in his hands. He took off at a run to greet the archaeologist. When the dog arrived at Chaz's chair he bumped the man's elbow with his nose to get his attention. Chaz looked up in surprise. When he saw Menlo he knew the time travelers had returned.

"I'm so glad to see you," he said as he stood to greet his friends. "You will not believe what happened here while you were gone."

"We have a pretty good idea," Allie replied. "But tell us the story anyway." She and the others examined the line of people standing around the shuttles. Like Menlo, the crews knew they were no threat and turned their attention back to Chaz and his story.

"If you remember, I protected my archaeologists by having them work in shifts. A shift could only work one day in the trench," Chaz began. "Then, they had to take a day off. That way, no one went into the trance. We kept digging around the domed building until we reached a door. Then, we stopped for the night. We planned on opening the door when we started work again in the morning. When we woke up, half of us were tied to our beds, and the people who had been in the dig that day were in a trance. During the night, they had taken the rest of us prisoner.

"The weirdest thing was the three people who had appeared overnight. There were two women and a man. They were beautiful." Chaz noticed the expressions on his friends' faces. "Do you know these people?" he asked in surprise. "They called themselves the Triumvirate."

"We have met them," Allie answered. "Go on. What happened next?"

"The three started singing," Chaz continued. "The rest of us went into the trance, everyone but me."

"That's weird," Nick said. "You and Carolus Nukium are the only people who don't go into the trance."

"Who is Carolus Nukium?" Chaz asked.

"Just someone we met in the past," Jen answered. She didn't think it was an important detail.

"Carolus? Ha," Chaz laughed. "I haven't heard that name in years. When I was studying Anthropology at UNH I learned that Carolus is an ancient way of saying my name – Charles. Chaz is just my nickname."

Mike's eyes opened like saucers. "Charles Nukium. Charles Newcomb!" he said to the others. "Get it?" he asked. "Carolus means Charles. Over time, Nukium got shortened to Newcomb. Chaz is a descendant of Carolus Nukium. He carries the gene. That's why he doesn't go into the trance. That means Carolus Nukium made it. He escaped. He married a cave woman and had a son he named Carolus. He developed the tradition of naming a son Carolus in every generation. Over time, Carolus was changed to Charles and Nukium was shorted to Newcomb. That's why we keep running into all these Charles Newcombs. They're all Carolus' descendants. He carried out his plan!"

They others stood silent, taking time to digest this discovery. For 12,000 years Carolus' family had marked their sons who carried the special gene by naming one of them Charles. They were standing with a direct descendent of the man they had found crying on the steps of the domed building, the man whose sail they had seen on the horizon. Chuck Newcomb, the World War II flyer was Carolus' descendant. So was Junior

Newcomb, the civil rights lawyer. So was Mr. Newcomb, their music teacher. So was Dr. Newcomb, their Ethics teacher and Chaz's father. So were Charlie Newcomb, the hippie from the future, and his infant son Charles.

Chaz didn't understand all this talk about a guy named Carolus Nukium and genes. What did Mike mean that Carolus Nukium had made it? Where did he go? Chaz lost interest and changed the subject back to the events at the dig. "The Triumvirate was armed," he said. "They carried spears with points made of polished granite. They looked razor sharp. I was unarmed and couldn't defend myself."

"They must have made their weapons while waiting for the city to rise out of the sea," Mike said. "They made spears because those are the only weapons they know about. They copied what the cavemen had. Still, spears can be very dangerous. We will need to be careful."

"The Triumvirate questioned me," Chaz continued.

"They questioned you?" Mike asked. "Where did they learn to speak English?" The others shrugged. "They are very clever," Mike concluded.

"They wanted to know where they were. I wouldn't tell them. So, they asked the transport pilots. Those guys were in a trance, but they were still able to answer questions. They told the Triumvirate about the transports. The three were amazed that we are able to fly. The pilots told them about time travel. That really excited them. They said if they combined our technology with theirs, they could not be stopped."

"Where are they now?" Jen asked.

"They went to the Time Institute," Chaz answered.

"This is bad," Mike added with a look of concern on his face. "If they get their hands on a time craft, they can go anywhere, any time. We won't know where or when they went. We won't be able to find them. Who knows what damage they could do?"

"Nick," Patrick said with worry in his voice. "Cut the two craft apart. We don't have to worry about getting lost any more. We're in our own time." When Nick and Lenore were done severing the duct tape, they carefully peeled the strips from the craft. The Auckland and the CT 9225 looked like new. Patrick opened his craft's door and stepped inside. The others watched him through the open door as he talked to his craft. He rubbed the cabin walls like a cowboy would rub his horse when he greeted the animal.

"Nick, Lenore, reinstall my human interface panel," he said to the pair of engineers.

While Patrick and Nick were busy in the CT 9225, Jen said to Mike, "We'll take Chaz with us. Meet us back at the Time Institute." Mike grimaced. He didn't like the idea of Chaz being with Allie. However, this was not the time to get jealous or make a fuss.

"I don't know if those guys will let me go," Chaz said, jerking his thumb at the hypnotized archaeologists and geologists with linked arms.

"Don't worry about them," Allie said, taking Chaz by the arm and tugging him toward the Auckland. "They have been ordered to keep you away from the transports. They don't care if you leave in another craft. They'll only do what they were told." Mike saw Allie take Chaz's arm. He turned away in anger as his old jealousy returned.

The two craft left the island and headed north to New Hampshire. While in flight Patrick turned on the University of New Hampshire radio station. He and his friends were surprised to hear the Triumvirate singing. "Oh no!" Mike said. "They're using our broadcasting system the same way they used the tubes under Atlantis. We're going to find everyone at the Time Institute in a trance."

Patrick contacted the Auckland and told Jen to turn on station WUNH. She did. Just like the boys, the Auckland's crew understood they had a problem back home. Meanwhile, Mike scanned the radio dial and found all the other stations were still broadcasting their normal programs. "The Triumvirate has only taken over UNH," Mike said. "That's why they're not on the other stations yet. I bet they've gone to Durham to get a time craft. If they take over UNH and the Time Institute, they'll have all they need. They'll be unstoppable. Soon, they'll have the whole world in a trance."

Mike stopped turning the dial when he heard a voice calling "Mayday! Mayday!" The boys recognized the international distress call. Mayday means someone is in trouble and needs help. "Mayday! Mayday!" the voice repeated. The boys recognized the speaker. It was Dr. Newcomb. He was using the Time Institute's communication system.

Mike immediately understood what had happened. "Dr. Newcomb has Carolus' gene," he said. "So, he's protected against the singing. He witnessed what is going on at the Institute and has hidden himself in the MacDonald Center. We have to rescue him. He can help us stop the Triumvirate."

Speaking ship to ship, Patrick told Jen what Mike had learned. He asked her to take the Auckland to UNH. There, her crew was to shut down the radio and put an end to the daily singing. Without that, people would eventually come out of the trance. Meanwhile, the CT 9225 would find Dr. Newcomb.

As the two craft reached Durham, they split up. The Auckland flew to UNH while the CT 9225 landed on the MacDonald Center's front lawn. The boys recognized the scene that greeted them. A row of hypnotized teachers and cadets blocked the building's entrance. They had their arms linked and their legs overlapping. They stared straight ahead. The boys knew many of the people in the line. Still, they were surprised when they spotted Rabbi Cohen. "Oh no," Nick whispered. "Not the rabbi."

As the boys approached the line blocking the doorway, Patrick wondered how he would get through it. He couldn't bring himself to bowl over people he knew so well. At last he said, "Give me a hand, Nick." Together the two approached Rabbi Cohen. "How are you doing, Rabbi?" Patrick asked. Each time traveler took the man under an arm. Together, they lifted him off the ground and gently placed the hypnotized rabbi to one side. Patrick waved to Mike and the CT 9225's crew passed through the hole in the line created by the missing rabbi.

As they entered the door Mike reminded his friends, "Chaz said the Triumvirate has spears. Spears seem primitive to us, but they are deadly weapons. Remember, the Neanderthals and the modern humans living in caves kill mammoths with nothing more than sharp stones attached to the ends of long sticks. We're defenseless. The Triumvirate's spears can do us a lot of damage."

"How can the Triumvirate be here if we heard singing on the radio?" Patrick asked. "They can't be in two places at one time."

"They must have made a recording," Nick answered.

The boys did not know where in the building Dr. Newcomb was hiding. They would have to search systematically. They started on the first floor. As they walked along the hallway they looked into each room. Next, they climbed the stairs and did the same thing on the second floor. They did not realize that the Triumvirate was also doing the same thing, only the three Atlanteans were ahead of them and already on the third floor. The Triumvirate had also heard the Mayday distress call. They knew someone in the building was not in a trance and was calling for help. They had to find him and stop him before he ruined their plan.

The three Atlanteans discovered Dr. Newcomb in Room 307. He was speaking into a microphone with his back to the door, still sending out his Mayday call. The Triumvirate burst into the room. "Stop!" Congrata commanded. The man at the microphone turned to look at the speakers. They were young and beautiful. They looked so much alike there was no doubt they were triplets, and there was no doubt they were not in a trance. There was also no doubt about their intent. They were here to stop him.

Dr. Newcomb was surprised at the seeing the Atlanteans. The three Atlanteans were stunned and shocked at seeing Dr. Newcomb. "Carolus Nukium!" Lexitus exclaimed. "Carolus Nukium, what are you doing here? How did you....? No matter. You will not stop us again. Remember, what I said when we last met? I will do it now and I will do it with pleasure."

"I'm Dr. Charles Newcomb of the Time Institute," the man replied. "I am not Carolus Nukium. I don't know Carolus Nukium. Who is he?"

"Do you think you can fool us that easily?" Exeta demanded. She spat out the words in scorn.

"I warned you, Carolus," Lexitus said approaching the small Time Institute teacher. The Atlantean held his spear in front of him. He placed the spear point close to the teacher's stomach. Suddenly, he jerked the spear back and shoved it forward. Dr. Newcomb's eyes opened wide like he had been surprised. He gave out a soft moan and fell to the floor.

At that moment the CT 9225's crew burst through the doors. The Triumvirate didn't have enough time to turn before the three times travelers were on top of them. Mike and Nick snatched the spears from the Congrata and Exeta and shoved the two small women out of the way. Patrick grabbed Lexitus' collar with his left hand and the man's waist with his right. Patrick's strength surprised even him. In his anger and rage, he lifted Lexitus off the ground and threw him across the room. The small Atlantean slammed into the far wall and fell to the floor. He was not unconscious. He had just had the wind knocked out of him.

Patrick picked up the man's spear and strode over to him. He placed the point of the spear on Lexitus' throat. Slowly, ever so slowly, Patrick put pressure on the spear. At first, the point pushed in Lexitus' skin, making a dimple. Then, as Patrick slowly added more pressure the needle-sharp point broke the skin and a small line of blood ran down the man's neck. The man's eyes opened wide in horror. He knew his own end was very close and his body shook with fear. He tried to control his shaking, as it only pressed his neck harder against the spear point. Mike and Nick held the two women and watched Patrick as he slowly finished off the man who had murdered their friend. They had no intention of stopping Patrick. This was justice. Lexitus was getting what he deserved.

At that moment, Jen burst through the door, followed by Allie and Lenore. From the look on Patrick's face Jen knew he was about to kill the man on the ground. "Patrick, Stop!" she screamed. Patrick just kept on pushing the spear, slowly, ever so slowly. He wanted this to hurt. He wanted this man to die in drawn out, painful agony. He wanted him to have plenty of time to contemplate what he had done.

Jen grabbed the spear and pulled the point away from the man's neck. This snapped Patrick out of his rage. He looked at Jen and tears erupted in his eyes. "He killed Dr. Newcomb," Patrick sobbed. The tears flowed like streams down his cheeks as he yelled at the top of his voice, "He killed Dr. Newcomb!" Patrick dropped his head backward so he looked at the ceiling. He screamed a mindless howl that was composed of raw pain and rage. Then, Patrick put his hands over his eyes and sobbed.

As soon as they had entered the room Allie and Lenore ran to Dr. Newcomb's lifeless body. Allie put her hands on the teacher's neck to feel for a pulse. She looked up at the others and sadly shook her head. The spear had done its job. Tears filled the eyes of the other five time travelers. The two Atlantean women had terror in their eyes. Lexitus lay on the floor with his hand on his throat. He still shook with fear. Beaten, the three had no fight left in them. No longer in control, they had no courage. In fact, they had become whimpering cowards.

Patrick went to his teacher and carefully picked up his limp body. He gently placed the dead man on the conference table. They had met with Dr. Newcomb at this table so many times. Patrick folded the man's hands on his chest and closed his half-open eyes. Except for the blood stain on his chest, Dr. Newcomb looked like he was asleep. Lenore found a cloth and covered her teacher.

"That was not Carolus Nukium," Mike said to the three Atlanteans, who huddled together in fear. "That was our friend, Dr. Charles Newcomb. You killed our friend, not your enemy." The three Atlanteans still cowered, but there was no look of regret in their eyes. They were not sorry. They were only worried about themselves, not about the man they had killed, or the pain they had caused his friends.

Nick went back to the CT 9225 and returned with his tool bag. He pulled out a roll of duct tape and tied the Atlanteans' hands behind their backs. He put strips of tape over their mouths. "We don't want them to start singing again," he explained to the others. "We have to wait a couple of days for everyone to come out of their trance. In the meantime, this will keep them under control, and quiet."

When the Time Institute people became their normal selves again, the boys turned the three Atlanteans over to Security. "They're dangerous," Mike explained to the full-sized men in blue uniforms. "They have to sing together to put people in a trace. So, keep them separate. Whatever you do, leave that duct tape on their mouths." Security took the Atlanteans to the UNH Medical Center where they would be examined.

Next, they met with Rabbi Cohen who was grieving for his dead friend. "I feel so guilty," the rabbi told the two crews. The time travelers looked surprised. Why did the rabbi feel responsible for what happened? "You lost a precious minute moving me out of the line," he explained. "If not for me, you could have arrived in time to save Charles."

"That is not your fault," Allie said soothingly. "You didn't ask to go into a trance. It was done to you. You could not resist."

"I know," the Rabbi answered. "I know. But part of my brain keeps screaming at me, accusing me of being responsible. I know it will pass. But right now, my guilt only makes my loss more painful. I miss my friend so much!" The rabbi burst into tears. The crews put their arms around him and gave him a tender and loving group hug. All the time travelers cried along with their teacher.

The Time Institute honored Dr. Newcomb by burying him in front of the MacDonald Center next to Dr. MacDonald. In coming months, a statue of the beloved teacher and dean of students was erected next to the statue of Dr. MacDonald. In these ways the teacher was recognized as a man of equal importance in the history of time travel.

At the funeral, the crews sat with Chaz and Mrs. Newcomb and Rabbi Cohen and Mrs. Cohen. After the funeral when all the people had gone, the crews told the others the story of their mission to Atlantis. They told how they had met Carolus Nukium, who looked just like his descendant Dr. Newcomb. They explained that Carolus had a gene mutation that protected him from the singing. They told how Carolus had escaped and gone to live with the modern humans. They explained Carolus' plan for every generation of his family to name a son Carolus, a name that in time changed to Charles. "I will keep up that tradition," Chaz promised. "I will name a son Charles in honor of my father, in honor of Carolus, in honor of all the Charles Newcombs who have done brave things." Mike saw Chaz glance at Allie. He knew what Chaz was asking with his eyes. Was Allie interested in being the mother of the next Charles Newcomb? Allie did not notice the glance. Mike let out a silent sigh of relief.

"Why did the island rise out of the sea?" Rabbi Cohen asked. "Did it happen on its own, or was it caused by the earth's plates moving? How did the Triumvirate survive all that time?"

"We're not sure," Mike explained. "This is my theory. The Triumvirate's vault was a stasis chamber. They had a technology that put them to sleep and kept them from aging. They made a mistake, or something went wrong. Instead of sleeping for a short time, they were in the chamber for 12,000 years. Meanwhile, the world around them changed. Modern humans spread around the globe and developed civilization. We created our own technology.

"I guess an earthquake shook the stasis chamber and awakened the Triumvirate. Then, they caused Atlantis to rise again. That was why the island came up out of the sea. They never expected that their city would be covered in mud and they wouldn't be able to get out of the building. As you dug deeper, Chaz, they heard you. They started singing to hypnotize anyone outside. I'm sure they were surprised when they finally opened their chamber and found a bunch of archaeologists and geologists. Once they learned from the hypnotized pilots they were in a new world, they quickly developed a new plan. We know the rest."

Several days later the crews met with Rabbi Cohen in Room 307. The time travelers were silent as they looked around the room. They remembered all too clearly what had happened the last time they were in here. "We have a problem on our hands," Rabbi Cohen told the six young people. "The Institute asked me to meet with you, as you dealt with a similar problem with Lt. Chuck Newcomb and Ensign Dubois. We have three Atlanteans at the UNH Medical Center, and we don't know what to do with them. We can't return them to Atlantis. If they went back and the Triumvirate created its empire, history would change. Atlantis was destroyed. That is its sequence and it must remain that way. As you know, the Triumvirate will not age outside their own time. That means we can't keep them here, and we can't take them to any other time. It would be cruel to make them live forever. And, we must never forget they are very dangerous. We have to put them where they can do no harm. Do you have any ideas?"

"I do," Mike announced. "We take them back to their time, just not to Atlantis." Everyone was surprised at this suggestion. "Remember the Neanderthals?" Mike continued. "During the Triumvirate's time they are dying out. They are on their way to extinction. We can take the Triumvirate to the Neanderthal cave we found, and leave them there. They can live with the Neanderthals. They will live their normal lifetimes and then die. That will be the end of the Triumvirate. If they change any Neanderthal sequences, it won't matter. Neanderthals go extinct. There would be no Chaos because their sequences end. All our problems will be taken care of. Of course, time crews should check up on the Triumvirate from time to time, just to be sure they are behaving."

"It's a plan," the Rabbi announced. "I will present your idea to the Institute. I am sure they will approve it. Will you two crews return the Triumvirate to the Neanderthals?" Jen and Patrick nodded in agreement.

The crews divided the Triumvirate between the two craft, just in case they tried to escape or put up a fight. The boys were the strongest so, they took Lexitus and Congrata. Exeta went in the Auckland. Outside the Neanderthal cave, Mike explained their fate to the three Atlanteans. "Welcome to your new life," he said. "Make friends with the short, redheaded people who live in that cave. They will make sure you are fed and warm. However, they will insist that you help out, that you make yourselves productive." The three Atlanteans sulked. "This is a pretty good deal," Mike added. "Other times in history, you would have paid with your own lives for having killed someone. You get to live. Our friend is still dead."

The two time craft disappeared as the three Atlanteans tramped through the snow toward the cave.

CHAPTER THIRTEEN
RECOVERY

Back at the Time Institute, after dropping off the Triumvirate, Mike told his friends, "I can't go back home right now. If I have to sit in class, I'll go crazy. I can't bear the thought of doing homework. I need some time to get over Dr. Newcomb." The others agreed. "I want to stay here for a while too," Nick added. Patrick nodded to say he felt the same way. The girls agreed and said they couldn't imagine doing any missions right now either. The six time travelers met with Rabbi Cohen. He said he would arrange for the Auckland's crew to take time off from work. He reminded the boys they were a time crew and were always welcome to stay at the Time Institute, as long as they wanted.

The crews returned to the crew quarters and assembled in the girls' apartment. They spent hours sitting silently. That afternoon Lenore announced, "Being in Durham keeps reminding me of Dr. Newcomb. Can we go somewhere else?"

"I agree," Jen added. "I don't want to think about anything. I want to go somewhere I can clear my mind. I want to sit and just stare at the sky. Everything else hurts too much."

"It was peaceful on that hillside in northern Spain," Allie answered. "We spent some pleasant days there before we went to Atlantis." The others agreed. That was a nice spot, and going back there would help them recover from losing Dr. Newcomb. The crews packed their two craft with the things they would need for a long camping trip.

The CT 9225 and the Auckland arrived on the hillside overlooking the olive grove. About a week had passed since they were last there. In his or her mind each crew member recalled the events that had occurred in that short time. From that spot, they had located the sequence of the Neolithic young man who asked his girl to marry him. Starting at his birth, they had tracked his woman ancestors' sequences back many thousands of years. They had found a tribe of Neanderthals and discovered that this species of humans had endured a lot longer than believed. They had found Atlantis. They had spent three days programming the helmets, and then visited with the pilgrims. Next, they tested the helmets by letting Mike go into a trance. A couple of days later they met Carolus Nukium. They had watched him escape as Atlantis sank into the sea. They returned home to find Chaz being held prisoner by his hypnotized team of archaeologists. They had heard the Triumvirate singing on the radio and had hurried to the Time Institute and UNH. They had found Dr. Newcomb's lifeless body and captured the

Triumvirate. They had waited while all the people at the Institute came out of their trance. They had attended Dr. Newcomb's funeral. Last, they had taken the Triumvirate to the Neanderthal cave. So much had happened in one short week. Time travel does mess with the mind.

The crews camped and rested. They spent lots of time lying on the grass watching clouds drift across a deep-blue sky. They watched the sun sparkle on the ocean. They watched the breezes rustle the leaves on the olive trees. At night they watched the stars, bright points of light on a black velvet background. They took walks, sometimes alone, sometimes with someone else.

They cried a lot, several times a day. They cried every time the pain of losing Dr. Newcomb became too great. When that happened the time travelers hugged Menlo for comfort. Menlo didn't know why his friends were in pain. But he knew, and was happy to be with them and to help. He lapped away their tears. He watched them with his sad brown eyes, eyes that seemed sadder because of his friends' sadness.

As the weeks passed, the time travelers cried less. They began to leave the hillside to visit other places. They went to the ocean and walked on the beach. They even waded in the water. It no longer bothered them to be around people. They walked through the town. One afternoon, Jen suggested they have lunch in a small restaurant. After lunch, on the way back up the hill Nick said, "We're in northern Spain. I thought people here spoke Spanish. They didn't. Whatever language they were talking sounded strange."

"That was Basque," Mike explained. "Remember I told you about the Indo-European language. It was spoken thousands of years ago. All other European languages were developed from it, all except Basque. Basque is a mystery. Scholars don't know where it came from. The only people in the world who speak Basque live in this corner, where Spain and France meet."

One day a couple of months later Mike went walking with Allie. He noticed the pain caused by losing his friend and teacher had changed. It reminded him of the time he broke his ankle. For a long time, his ankle ached and ached. It hurt so much that sometimes he cried. A couple of weeks later, it still hurt, but not like before. That was when he found he could bend it – very carefully and slowly, but he could bend his ankle. Soon, he was able to put weight on his foot, and even walk. He limped, but he could walk. In time, the ankle became strong and he could run on it. His ankle was healed.

Mike realized the same thing was happening now. The pain of Dr. Newcomb's death didn't hurt as much as when they came to the hillside. Back then, he and his friends had cried and cried because the pain was so intense. Now, his heart still hurt, but not as much as before. He knew what was happening. He knew his heart was beginning to heal, just like his ankle had healed. He told his friends what he had discovered. They all agreed that as time passed they too hurt less.

The two crews began to talk about their feelings. They reminisced about Dr. Newcomb. They remembered the first time they had met him. He had walked into the classroom at the MacDonald Center. "I remember the joke you made," Patrick said to Mike. "This is our second first day of school this year."

"Remember how Dr. Newcomb came into the class?" Allie asked. "He put his papers on his desk and he became so serious. He told us his name and then said, 'This is the most important class you will take at the Time Institute. Our ethics code controls all your actions as time travelers. Whether you are trained as pilots, science observers, or engineers, you must always act the way I teach you.'"

"He was so surprised when he saw us in Fixer uniforms," Nick recalled. "He actually forgot what he was saying."

"I wasn't in your cadet class," Lenore added. "Did he walk back and forth behind his desk, looking at the floor? Did his face go from serious to smiling as he waited for you to ponder what he had just said? You know, he was always smiling. It was like his smile was painted on his face. Did he tell you guys 'All people are tied together by our common humanity? Your humanity ties you to everyone else living now, or who has ever lived?'" The others nodded. Yes, Dr. Newcomb had said the same things when they took his Ethics class. Tears filled Lenore's eyes as she remembered her teacher.

"He taught us important stuff," Jen added. "He taught us that we must never consider ourselves better than any other human being. Remember he said, 'Treat them with the same care and respect you would want for yourself, and for the people you love.' I think we have done that, don't you?" she asked her friends. "I think we did what he taught us."

"I think Dr. Newcomb was proud of us," Mike said. "We were good students and he was happy how we turned out. I think he really liked us. I know I loved him. I miss him so much." Mike burst into tears. Allie hugged him. Menlo lapped his face.

As the days passed the crews talked more and more about Dr. Newcomb. When they had first arrived on the hillside, just thinking about him hurt more than they could stand. Now, talking about their teacher made them feel better. Nick remembered when Dr. Newcomb met his ancestor, Lt. Chuck Newcomb. They were all at the UNH Medical Center. "Can you imagine how weird that must have been for him?" The time travelers all laughed at the memory.

"Do you realize we just laughed?" Allie asked. "I haven't laughed since…, you know, that day. That was six months ago. It felt good to laugh. I think Dr. Newcomb would have wanted us to laugh. He would have wanted us to go on living our lives. He would want us to always remember him, but he would want us to go on living. I think I'm ready for that."

When the crews returned to the Time Institute they met with Rabbi Cohen. "I'm glad you are all back and feeling better," he told them. "Miss Tymoshenko. A request for a mission came through last week from a music researcher at UNH. I told the researcher you were on vacation and it might take a while. If you are up for it, I will arrange for you, and Miss Smith, and Miss Canfield to meet with her." The Auckland's crew all nodded. Yes, a mission would be a good thing.

"Mr. Weaver, you will be interested in this," Rabbi Cohen said to Patrick. "Do you remember the papers you took from the desk in the domed building before the Triumvirate destroyed Atlantis? They have been studied. Your helmets learned the Atlantean language and that has been studied too. We have solved one of history's mysteries and created another. It turns out Atlantean is the same as the Basque language. Now we know where Basque came from. However, we also know Atlantis was destroyed. We can't figure out how the language got to the corner of Spain and France."

"That's easy," Mike announced. "The only Atlantean to survive was Carolus Nukium. He must have settled where France and Spain meet. He taught his children to speak Atlantean and they spoke that language with their children. The language stayed in that area all these years. Carolus Nukium didn't just pass on his gene to his children. He passed on his language too."

"Fascinating," Rabbi Cohen replied, pausing a minute to think about Mike's conclusion. "Oh, there's some other news that will interest you," he said to the crews. "It involves a friend of yours. Chaz Newcomb is getting married. He's engaged to one of the archaeologists that worked on the dig with him, a woman named Sandy. His friend Will the geologist is going to be Best Man." The others all smiled and nodded. This was nice and they were happy for Chaz. Mike breathed a silent sigh of relief.

After meeting with Rabbi Cohen the boys were ready to leave for home. They walked the girls back to the crew quarters. On the way, Mike said, "We know Carolus Nukium left behind his gene and his language. I think the Triumvirate left something behind as well." The others looked at him, wondering what it could be. "There's an ancient legend about mermaids, people from the sea who could hypnotize sailors with their singing. The Greeks called these mermaids the Sirens. It's where we get the name for our band. What we know about the Triumvirate sounds a lot like the legend of the Sirens. If they were the origin of that story, we're all connected to Congrata, Lexitus, and Exeta in a really weird way. Our band is named for them." As they walked no one spoke. They all pondered Mike's idea.

When the two crews arrived at the crew quarters they all hugged and kissed goodbye. The girls each took a turn hugging Menlo.

The boys hid the CT 9225 in the woods and returned to Mike's house. As they walked up the path to the Castleton's gingerbread cottage, Menlo ran ahead and scratched at the door. He had not been home for more than six months and he was anxious to see the rest of his family. He wanted to eat from his food bowl and sleep in his bed. Mrs. Castleton opened the door for the dog and greeted Mike and his friends. "Where are the girls?" she asked in surprise.

"We walked them home," Mike told his mother. Technically, he was not lying. Before returning to their own time they had walked with the girls to their home at the crew quarters.

"Nick and Patrick," Mrs. Castleton asked next. "Do you boys want to stay for dinner?"

"I can't," Patrick answered. "We're visiting my grandmother tonight. My father is going to pick me up soon."

"Thanks," Nick said. "I have a History paper due on Monday. I promised my parents I would finish it tonight. They're going to pick me up too."

After Nick and Patrick had left, Mrs. Castleton sat at the kitchen table with Mike. Menlo was asleep with his head on her foot. "Allie and her friends are very nice," she told her son. "Your father and I liked them a lot. I hope you will bring them by again."

"I think we will," Mike said. "Nick, Patrick, and I like them a lot too. So," he asked. "What are we doing tonight?"

"Your father is on another one of his old movie kicks," Mrs. Castleton answered, rolling her eyes. "For tonight he picked one of those dumb adventures from the early 1960s. You know the kind with the really bad special effects. At least we'll have a night together as a family. I'll make popcorn."

"I like that idea. Those dumb old movies are funny to watch," Mike laughed. "Which one is it?

"Atlantis: The Lost Continent."

ABOUT THE AUTHOR

Mike Dunbar began writing as a 19-year old cub reporter. Since then, he has published seven books and written more magazine articles than he can remember. His name has been on the mastheads of three national magazines. He has been a newspaper and magazine columnist, and an editor. He has hosted a radio and a television show. He is in demand as a seminar speaker. He lives in Hampton, NH with his family. He operates and teaches at The Windsor Institute, a school that specializes in handmade Windsor chairs, He blogs atmikedunbar.tumblr.com, windsorchairs.tumblr.com, andthewindsorinstitute.com/blog. He tweets at @Castleton series.

MORE BOOK
BY MIKE DUNBAR

BOOK 6 THE BREAKOUT
DUE OUT JUNE 15TH, 2014

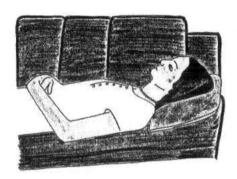

CHAPTER ONE
ABDUCTION

Jorge and Jane Montez were driving home to the small isolated town of Lyndeborough, New Hampshire. It was a Sunday night in November, 1969. Lyndeborough is on top of a small mountain, so most of the ride is uphill. It was pitch black as the couple carefully wove their way along a winding country road. There was no moon and the two people could see only what passed through the beams of the car's headlights. It was mid-month, and leaves that had been brilliant autumn colors only weeks ago had fallen from the trees. This allowed stars to wink occasionally through leafless branches. Sometimes, the headlight beams would reflect off the eyes of some critter feeding near the edge of the tar road, a road that was not quite wide enough for two lanes. The couple would see two eerie, green dots. Then, the animal would turn and run into the brown grass and other dead plants alongside the pavement. Otherwise, the road was deserted.

"We shouldn't have stayed so late at Aunt Sue's," Jane said to her husband. Jorge looked briefly at his wife and then returned his attention to his driving. If he was to stay on a country road this narrow, on a night this dark, he had to focus.

"You're the one who wouldn't leave," he replied. Jorge was from the Dominican Republic and his native language was Spanish. He spoke English with a strong accent. Jane had grown up in Lyndeborough and had a rural New Hampshire accent. In the 1960s a mixed couple – an Anglo woman and a husband of African descent would have been outcasts in most parts of the United States. However, every small New Hampshire town is home to lots of odd and unusual characters. So, rural New Hampshire has always been tolerant of those who are different. Even though Jorge was an outsider and a black-skinned foreigner, Lyndeborough was quick to accept him when he married a local girl.

"I know," Jane sighed. "But I was having so much fun with my sisters. Look," she said pointing at the car's dashboard clock, "it's already 9:15. We won't be home until 10:00. It will be 10:30 before we get into bed. Then, we're up again at 5:00. We'll be dragging tomorrow."

"There's a light in the sky," Jorge said, pointing through the windshield. "It can't be a star. It's much too bright." The light Jorge had spotted disappeared among a tangle of naked tree limbs. Jane bent forward to look out the windshield, but did not see what her husband was gesturing at. "It's gone," Jorge told her. A moment later he saw it again. "There," he said, pointing and slowing the car so Jane would have time to get a glance. Again, the light disappeared behind the canopy of limbs overhanging the road.

Jorge didn't think of the bright light again. Driving on this dark road was too demanding. He had travelled it many times and knew all the twists and turns. However, out in the country at night, lots of things could be in the road: deer, moose, bear. Even cows and horses occasionally escaped from neighboring farms. Hitting a large animal would damage, and even wreck their 1964 Ford station wagon. The car would knock the legs out from under a tall animal such as a moose or a horse. The animal would roll up on the car's hood and a half ton of flesh would crash through the windshield. Every year in New Hampshire several people die that way.

Five minutes later, Jorge saw the light again. This time, it was even larger and brighter than before. "There it is again,' he said insistently, "just off to the right through that tree." He pointed in its direction to help Jane find it.

This time Jane caught a glimpse before it disappeared in the branches. "I saw it," she said. "Is it an airplane? The lights on planes are that bright when they land at the Boston airport."

"I don't think so," Jorge replied. "It would have to be a big plane to be that bright. What would a plane that size that be doing here in the middle of nowhere? It could be a B52 bomber from Pease Air Force Base over in Portsmouth. But a B52 shouldn't be that low. The base is too far away for a plane to be making a landing approach. Besides, we would be able to hear the engines." The couple didn't say any more as they drove. However, each glanced up from time to time. Judging from the plane's path, it could pass right over their road and they didn't want to be frightened by its roar. Being startled on a narrow, dark road at night is a good way for a driver to end up in a ditch.

Jorge steered the station wagon around a long curve. Even though he and Jane couldn't see it, they knew the road well, and were aware the forest had ended and to the right was a large apple orchard. The couple was stunned when they spotted a bright light in the orchard. The few people who lived in the area were farmers and they would not be out late on a Sunday night. They all went to bed at 8:00 and by now were sound asleep. It was mid-November. By early October all the apples had been picked and the leaves had long since fallen off those short, well pruned fruit trees. Until next spring, the orchard would be normally unattended by humans, and only provide a habitat for wildlife.

There was only one explanation for the bright light; someone was jacking deer. Jacking deer is a form of poaching and is illegal. It is also unfair to the deer. People who do it go into a field with a spotlight and shine the light on a deer that is feeding. The deer is blinded by the light and freezes. Then, the poacher shoots the defenseless animal.

Jorge stopped the car and pulled over onto the shoulder as far as he could. He wanted his station wagon off the road, but needed to avoid getting stuck in the soft dirt. He reached in front of his wife and opened the glove compartment. He pulled out a pistol. "What are you doing?" Jane demanded with alarm.

"Last year the Lyndeborough town meeting elected me animal control officer," Jorge answered matter-of-factly. "Hunters are jacking deer and it is my duty to arrest them." He was out the door before Jane could protest. "Jorge," she yelled. "Are you crazy? You're going into a deserted orchard at night where people are committing a crime. What's to stop them from shooting you?" Her husband didn't respond, so she opened her door and followed after him. "Get back," Jorge yelled over his shoulder at his wife. Jane ignored him and broke into a trot to catch up with him.

Jane stirred. She was so deeply asleep her muscles wouldn't work. She couldn't even open her eyes. Drifting between sleep and wakefulness, she wondered where she was. She wasn't in bed. Without opening her eyes she could tell she was in a sitting position. Her back was upright and her knees were bent. Most of her weight was on her butt. Yes, she was sitting, maybe not up straight, but she was sitting. That confirmed she wasn't in bed. She drifted back to sleep, only to rise back to consciousness a minute later. She focused her attention on her eyelids and eventually summoned enough strength to force them open. She was in the passenger seat of their Ford station wagon. It was night. What was she doing here, her muddled mind wondered? Jorge. Where was Jorge? Twisting her head was like using her neck muscles to turn a boulder. It took every ounce of strength and determination she could muster. Even at that, her head turned ever so slowly, until at last she could see the driver's seat. There was Jorge, deep asleep with his head tilted backward, resting against the top of his seat back. He was even snoring.

With her head turned, Jane could also see the clock in the dashboard. Three o'clock…. Three o'clock! The shock of realizing the late hour sent a surge of energy through her and she shook off the last of the deep sleep that had paralyzed her muscles. "Jorge!" she called with alarm. "Jorge." Her husband stirred. "Jorge. Wake up," Jane insisted. She had regained use of her arms but felt like everything she did was in slow motion. It was a great endeavor just to reach over and put her hand on her husband's shoulder. With effort she shook him. "Jorge. Wake up!"

Jorge slowly opened his eyes. "Jorge," Jane said loudly. "We've fallen asleep. It's three in the morning and we're asleep by the side of the road.

"Huh?" Jorge grunted through the fog of deep sleep. "What? We did what?"

"We fell asleep. It's three in the morning. We've got to get up in two hours and go to work."

"Work?" Jorge said slowly and dully.

"Look at the clock!" Jane insisted. Peering through half-open eye lids, Jorge slowly turned his head toward the dashboard. When he saw the clock, his eyes popped fully open.

"Three o'clock!" he said in alarm, his voice louder because of the shock. "What are we doing here? How did we fall asleep?"

"We did stay late at Aunt Sue's," Jane said as she pondered her husband's question. "I had a glass of wine, but that was at supper. It was not enough to make me sleepy."

"I don't know what happened," Jorge answered. "But we had best get home and get what little good sleep we can. I am going to be exhausted in the morning."

As soon as they arrived home the couple went straight to bed. The alarm clock went off at 5:00 sharp and they struggled to get up and get dressed. They climbed back into their station wagon and drove down the mountain and into the nearby city of Nashua. Jorge dropped his wife off at her job. They kissed as they parted and confirmed that he would pick her up at 4:00 that afternoon. Neither mentioned the night before. Both were a little bit embarrassed about falling asleep beside the road and didn't want to discuss it.

A month went by. One afternoon Jorge picked up Jane in front of the office where she worked. "How was your day?" he asked.

"It was fine. How about yours?"

"I talked to the plant doctor," Jorge replied. His wife's head snapped as she turned to look at him. She was worried Jorge was ill. "It wasn't anything big," Jorge explained. "It's just that I've been worried a lot. I have this feeling that something bad is going to happen at any minute. When the phone rings, I worry that something will be wrong. I open my mail and I worry that each letter will bring a disaster. He checked me out. I'm fine, but my blood pressure is sky high. It was always normal before. He said it's stress and it's making me anxious. He recommended I use some of my vacation time. He suggested we go to Florida and that I sit on a beach and read a book."

"That may be a good idea," Jane answered. "I've been having strange dreams. I'm always trying to run away from something frightening. My legs won't work. I'm stuck and the danger is getting closer. Then, before whatever it is gets to me I wake up. I'm breathing hard and my heart is racing. Sometimes, I'm sweating. I told my sister. She said I'm having anxiety dreams. She says that type of dream means I'm feeling trapped. A vacation may be just what I need."

Jorge and Jane returned from Florida, but they were not tanned and rested. Their dreams and anxiety did not go away on vacation. In fact, they were getting worse. Now, Jorge was having dreams too and Jane was also anxious about bad things happening. When they got back to work, Jorge went to the company doctor again. The doctor suggested he and his wife visit a marriage counselor. Since they were both having the same problems, he suspected trouble in their marriage. He gave Jorge the name of a psychologist to call.

Jorge and Jane visited the psychologist several times. Each visit, they sat on the couch and talked about their marriage. The psychologist realized everything was fine between them. They loved each other. They enjoyed their lives. They were both healthy people. "Since you're both having similar troubles, I suspect something is going on that you are not aware of," the shrink told them. "I am going to suggest something very different from normal therapy. I am giving you the name of a hypnotist. I think that under hypnosis you may discover something deep, something hidden that is causing your problems."

The couple thought it a bit strange to visit a hypnotist for problems like dreams and anxiety, but they followed the psychologist's advice. The hypnotist was an older man. He spoke English with a slight French accent. He said he had come to America as a young man to study and had decided to stay. He listened patiently while Jorge and Jane explained why they were here. He wrote notes on a large pad.

Finally, he said, "There does seem to be some unknown cause to your problems. I don't know what it is, but I think it may be a painful experience you have both shared." Jorge and Jane looked at each other.

Jane's father had died a couple of years ago. That had been painful, but she couldn't see how it could bother Jorge enough to cause nightmares. "I want to work with each of you alone," he told Jorge and Jane. "I don't want one to know what the other has said under hypnosis. I'm afraid that your unconscious minds will influence each other. Let's make an appointment for next week."

Jane showed up at the hypnotist's office for her appointment. "Come in, Mrs. Montez," the man said warmly and quietly. "I want you to lie down on this couch. First take off your shoes and jewelry. Loosen any clothes that are tight. I want you to be completely comfortable." He turned off the lamps and drew a window shade to darken the room. "Now, Mrs. Montez, close your eyes," he said. At the same time, he turned on a tape recorder on the table next to him. This would make a record of the session that he and other medical professionals could study later. "I want you to listen to my voice." He was talking slowly and in a gentle sing-song way. "Stay connected to my voice. It will keep you connected with me while you fall asleep. You will not drift away if you always stay connected to my voice."

The hypnotist sat back in his chair and said, "I want you to relax completely. Listen to my suggestions. Every muscle in your body is relaxing. Feel them go limp. Start at your feet and slowly work up your legs. Make every muscle relax." He paused while Jane's mind worked slowly up her legs. She had held her feet together. He saw them fall gently away from each other so they formed a V. "Now, all the muscles in your stomach and chest, make them relax." Again he paused while she obeyed his suggestion. "Now, your arms. They do not work anymore. They hang by your sides." Jane's fingers curled slightly as her arms and hands went limp. "Finally, your head. All the muscles in your neck and jaw are relaxed." Jane's neck muscles went soft and her jaw fell forward so her mouth was slightly open.

"Now, I want you to focus on your breathing," the hypnotist said, his voice so soft it was just above a whisper. "Breath slowly. Inhale deeply, but don't hold your breath. Exhale. I want you to let out the air at the same speed you took it in. I want each in and out to take the same amount of time. Focus on making your breathing deep and even. Make it a smooth rhythm. Innnnn. Ouuuut. Innnnn. Ouuuut." Jane's chest rose and fell in a steady rhythm.

"Next, I want you to look at something far, far away," the hypnotist said softly. "It is small, just a point. I want you look at it and bring it into focus. Hold it in focus. Don't look away." He saw Jane's eyes roll upward as she obeyed his instructions. She was ready.

"Mrs. Montez," the hypnotist said. "Something is bothering you. I want you to call up that something. It is in your mind. Bring it forward so you can talk about it and describe it." Jane's breathing changed and began to come in short breaths. The hypnotist recognized this as a sign of fear. "Where are you, Mrs. Montez?" he asked.

"I'm at the apple orchard on Mountain Road," she said with fear in her voice.

"When is it?" the hypnotist asked.

"I don't know," Jane answered. "It's dark. Wait. I see it. We're coming home from Aunt Sue's. It's November. We were at my sister's birthday party in Nashua. We have stopped at the orchard because there's a light in it. They're jacking deer. Jorge is taking a pistol from the glove compartment. He's getting out of the car. 'Are you crazy? You're going out in a deserted field at night where people are committing a crime. What's to stop them from shooting you?'" she said to the image of Jorge she saw in her mind. "Jorge is walking into the field. I have to go with him."

A look of horror came over Jane's face and her eyes popped open. However, she didn't look at the hypnotist or his office. Her gaze was far away. She was still in the orchard and she was reviewing what happened that night. "Who are you? What are they, Jorge? These aren't hunters. Jorge, shoot. Shoot! Argghhh!"

"Relax Mrs. Montez," the hypnotist said calmly. "Let's take a short break. Return to your relaxed condition." Jane closed her eyes. She took a deep breath and gradually resumed her measured, steady breathing. Her mind had let go of the terror it had just relived. The hypnotist waited a while and began again. "Mrs. Montez, go back to where we stopped. You had told your husband to shoot. What do you see?"

"I don't know," Jane said. "It is dark. I don't see much. There are things... people... no, creatures here.

There is a group of them. I see their outlines against the light in the distance. Their faces are in shadow."

"Describe what you can see," the hypnotist told his patient.

"They are small, like kids in grade school. They have arms, but they are long like a monkey's. They reach to their knees. Their legs are long and thin. Their bodies are short and round. I can't make out anything else. It's too dark."

"What happens next?" the hypnotist asked.

"One of them is pointing at us like it has a gun. No, it looks more like a pen. A tiny spot of green light appears on my chest. I have fallen. I can't move. I can see. My eyes are open, but I can't move. I'm awake and I can't move. I hear some of these creatures behind me. Two more are beside me. They take me by the arms and pick me up. They put me down. My back is resting on something. It is a hard surface. I am level with the ground. I'm lying on some sort of platform. I can see out of the corners of my eyes. I am not on the ground any more. I am slightly above it. Now, I am moving away from the road into the orchard. The two figures walk beside me. They don't seem to be touching what I am lying on, but they seem to be guiding it. I notice the stars. The sky above the orchard is full of them." Jane's breathing became heavy again as her fear returned.

"If you're feeling frightened," the hypnotist said, "relax and we will wait a moment. Breathe deeply and evenly until you feel comfortable. Good. Good. Now, what is happening?"

"I'm going into something. Is it a building? No, it is something else. It is a room. I'm in a room. It's like a living room, but it's different. I see more creatures out of the corner of my eye. There must be at least six or seven. I can't be sure because I can't turn my head."

Jane stopped talking. "What is happening now?" the hypnotist asked.

"Nothing," Jane replied. "I'm just lying here. Wait. I see figures. They are putting something next to me. I think its Jorge. I can't call to him. My mouth won't open. I think it is Jorge. I think he is on a platform like I am. I can't be sure. If only I could turn my head." The woman went silent.

"Yes, yes." the hypnotist said. "What is happening now?"

"Nothing," Jane answered. "I am just waiting here."

"Good. Good," the hypnotist said to her. "I want to you move forward in time until something happens. Do you understand? Tell me the next thing that happens."

"They are back," Jane replied. "There are three of them. Two are standing over me on my right, and one on my left. They are looking down at me."

"Stop," The hypnotist said softly. "Before you tell me more of what is happening, tell me what the creatures look like in the light. Take a minute and examine them closely."

"They are small," Jane began. "About the size of school children. They have gray skin. They have large, oval eyes. I don't see any pupils or any whites. Their eyes are like black glass. They have small noses, so small they are no more than a bump in the middle of their faces. Their nostrils are bigger than their noses. Their mouths are very small too, and they have almost no chins. They don't have ears. They don't have hair. They don't have eyebrows. They are just smooth, gray skin.

"They are wearing clothes, but I can only see their shoulders. It seems to be a type of cloth, but it is shiny, like metal. One of the two on my right has its arm raised. I can see its hand. It only has three fingers. They are long and boney. Wait. One of the fingers turns inward like a thumb. Yes. He is using it like a thumb. He is holding something that looks like a ballpoint pen. He is using his third finger like a thumb."

Jane stopped talking. "Anything else about them?" the hypnotist asked.

"No, that's how they look," Jane replied.

"Next, I want you to tell me about anything else you notice. I know you can't move, but look upward. What do you see?"

"There are some objects on the ceiling over me," Jane said. "I don't know what they are. They may be equipment. One looks like something dentists use. I don't know what it is. It has a small shiny plate on it. Wait. It's shiny like a mirror. I can see myself. It's a tiny image, but I can see myself!"

"Is there anything unusual? Can you see anything besides yourself?" the hypnotist asked. Jane's story was so fascinating it was hard for him to remain calm and not get excited. He forced himself to speak softly and slowly. This detail was important. Jane had discovered a window that would allow her to see more of this strange place.

"I am not wearing any clothes," Jane answered. There was alarm in her voice. I can see from the top of my head to my belly button. They took my clothes. Why did they do that? I'm embarrassed."

"It's alright," the hypnotist said soothingly. "You're the only one who can see you. It's no different from seeing yourself in the mirror before stepping into the shower. Now, let's start again. What is happening?"

Jane's mind ceased staring at the image her memory seen in the shiny surface. Her subconscious began to relive the action again. "The figures are looking at me. They are not talking. One is pointing at my chest and drawing a line with its finger. Another traces a line in a different place. They act like they're talking, but their mouths aren't moving.

"They are doing something with that thing that looks like a pen. The one on the left is following the line that the other drew with his finger."

"If you look in the shiny metal," the hypnotist suggested, "can you see what they are doing? Jane's eyeballs rolled upward as if she were still on the platform and not on the hypnotist's couch. He watched her eyes as she tried to focus on the small reflected image of herself on the reflective metal.

Jane's body went stiff. She tried to struggle, but she was still in the hypnotic trance. Once again, her eyes opened in terror. She could not see the hypnotist's office, only the place in her memory. "Oh, My God!" she screamed in fear. The horror in her voice was blood curdling. "They have cut me open from my chin to my belly button! They have laid me open! I can see my insides!"

The hypnotists reacted quickly. "Mrs. Montez," he said firmly, taking control of the situation. "Mrs. Montez, breathe deeply. Focus on your breathing. Stay connected to my voice. Let your mind go blank. Relax.... Relax.... Relax." Jane went limp and her breathing became deep and steady.

After some time had passed the hypnotist said calmly, "Mrs. Montez, we know you have been cut open and you can see your insides. So, this cannot frighten you again. This time I want you to watch without fear and tell me what happens. Look at yourself in the shiny surface, but we know what you will see, so you will not be afraid. Now, what happens next?"

Jane was relaxed and talked about what she saw being done to her without any fear. "They have my body open but there is no blood. They are poking at my parts. I don't know what is what. Wait. I know that one. That's my heart. I can see it beating. Those two on the sides of it are lungs. They are getting bigger and smaller as I breathe. They have something that looks like a small egg carton. They are taking little pieces of my parts and putting the pieces in the sections of the container.

"Look at that," Jane said with a slight smile, as if what she saw amused her. "They just closed me up with that thing that looks like a pen. They drew it up from my belly button and I closed up like they were pulling a zipper." The hypnotist looked at Jane's neck where it was exposed above her collar. There was no scar.

Jane continued to describe the action. "Hmmm," she said with interest, but no fear. "They are going around my head with that pen-like thing." A moment later she added, "They have cut off the top of my head. I can see my brain. They seem to be putting things into it. They point at my brain, but they don't speak." Jane stopped talking.

"What is happening?" the hypnotist asked.

"Nothing," Jane answered. "They seemed to have put things in my brain, but they are just waiting." Some time passed. Jane started again. "Now, they are taking the things out of my brain. They must be very small objects. I cannot see what they look like. Oh!" she added with surprise. "They just put the top of my head back on and closed it up with that pen thing." She chuckled with amusement. "It's just like closing a zipper," she said.

"Go on," the hypnotist encouraged his patient. He looked at Jane's forehead. There was no scar there either.

"They seem to be done with me," Jane continued. "They are moving me back the way I came in. I'm outside again. Wait, I can see just a bit of the building I was in. I wish I could move my eyes. It's shiny and it's smaller than I thought. What I see looks like a bus, the kind people take when they go on long trips. It's wider than a bus, though. I can't see the whole thing, just the top part."

Jane continued to describe what was happening in her memory. "I'm back at the station wagon. They have opened the door. I can see Jorge in the driver's seat. His head is tilted back and he looks like he is asleep. They have put me in the passenger's side. I am in a sitting position, but I'm a bit slouched to one side. One is staring into my eyes......"

"Yes, Mrs. Montez," the hypnotist said with just a hint of impatience in his voice. This was so interesting he was a bit annoyed that she had stopped. "What is happening?"

"Nothing," Jane answered. "It's just black."

"Okay," the hypnotist said. "Go forward in your mind to the next thing you remember."

"Where am I?" Jane asked. "Oh, my body is like lead. It won't move. I can feel something with my butt. I am sitting. I think I'm in a car. I have to force my eyes open. It is so hard. Eyelids, open. I must fight to make them open. There. Yes, I'm in the car. There's the dashboard. I can see the clock. What!? It's three in the morning! What am I doing here?"

"Mrs. Montez," the hypnotist said. "You have returned to what you remember in your conscious mind. It is time for you to wake up. I will count to three and snap my fingers. That will be your signal. When you awake you will feel refreshed and you will remember nothing that you have told me. Now, one, two...."

Jane and Jorge sat in the hypnotist's office, not on the couch, but in arm chairs. It was their fourth visit. At the first appointment they had told the hypnotist their problems. At the second, he had hypnotized Jane. The third visit was Jorge's turn to be hypnotized. Now, the hypnotist had brought them together to tell them what he had discovered. He gave each a loose-leaf notebook with typewritten pages. "I had my secretary type up the conversations we had while you were hypnotized," he told the couple. "Take some time to read them." He waited.

When the two were through reading the hypnotist continued. "I don't know what to make of your stories. They are both the same. You describe the same creatures, the same room, and the same things happening to you. I don't know how or why you both have the same story. Either you read the same book, or watched the same movie, or... it really happened."

"I never read a book like this," Jorge said "or watched a movie like this." Jane nodded in agreement.

"That leaves the possibility that this really happened," the hypnotist said. "You may have had an experience with what the government calls Unidentified Flying Objects – UFOs. I think we should tell someone. I know the government denies these things, so they will cover up your story. I suggest we show the evidence to someone who will share it with the public, so they can decide. I think we should call a reporter from a newspaper. The wire services will spread your story around the country, and then the government can never cover it up." Jane and Jorge nodded. They agreed. They would talk to the press and tell their story.

OTHER BOOKS BY SOUL STAR PUBLISHING

The Price of Love, Book 3 in the Lore of Algoron Trilogy
By Gus Gallows

Love. A very human thing this... love. The softlings claimed it could bring such peace and joy, and yet it was also responsible for so much death and dismay. Phintomini, the copper dragon, was confused by the obvious paradox. He did not understand it and as it was with all things he did not understand, he would not rest until understanding was attained. He would learn of this thing called love, but not in the way of his previous lessons. It would not be from reading the ancient scrolls, or from his spying on the neighboring cities and townships. This time, his lesson would come from that of a simple, orphaned, elven child, and a kidnapped priestess. This time he would learn of love that, though freely given, comes with a powerful price. The Price   of Love.

Available in paperback and e-book formats at your favorite e-book or traditional retailer.

The Triangle,
Book 4 in The Castleton Series
by Mike Dunbar

For centuries ships and planes disappeared off the Florida coast never to be seen again: that is until two Navy flyers lost in 1945 while searching for Flight 19, pop up in Morocco 1,000 years before they were born. Their experience was so bizarre the aviators have suffered mental breakdowns. Discovered and rescued by the Auckland's crew -- Allie Tymoshenko, Jen Canfield, and Lenore Smith-- the two aviators become a problem for the Time Institute. The men were declared dead and their families went on living without them. They can't be returned to their own time without setting off Chaos. The Institute can't keep them in the future because they will never age. Patrick Weaver and his crew- Nick Pope and Mike Castleton- are enlisted to help discover what happened, only to find themselves trapped between dimensions in a place so weird it is beyond human understanding. To make matters worse, the place is full of lost people, long thought dead, with nowhere to go. Working with a 300 year old slave named Kwasi, the crews search for a solution.

Available in paperback and e-book formats at your favorite e-book or traditional retailer.

The Price of Dignity, Book 2 in the Lore of Algoron Series
By Gus Gallows

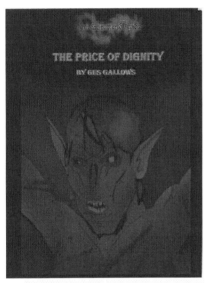

The gemstone mines of Golem's Tear were home and prison to the most detested race in all of Algoron; the filthy and despicable Goblins. Enslaved by the Dwarven Kingdom of Thaxanos, they lived and died at their masters' whims-that is until a few of the lowly creatures rose up from the filth, took up arms, and made their stand.

This is the story of the rise of Dolund'ir, the first Goblin Kingdom of Algoron, and those who pushed it gnawing and screaming into the world's light.

Angel's Dance
Book 2 in the Clear Angel
Chronicles
By Heidi Angell

Psychic Clear Angel hasn't seen or heard from her

one-time lover Detective Grant since their first case wrapped up six months ago, and that is perfectly fine with her! But when he shows up on her porch in the rain and in tears, she cannot hold her ground. No matter how she feels about Grant and her "gift", she can't ignore the visions already pouring in.

Grant knows that he is no good for Clear, and has respected the distance she has kept. But when his daughter goes missing and the Chicago police have no leads, he turns to Clear and her unique abilities.

This next adventure puts Grant and Clear in close quarters as they find themselves once again fighting their feelings for one another. Thrust into the dark underworld of performance art, they strive to track down a ballerina who keeps taunting Clear in her visions. As they delve deeper into one studio, the grisly visions that haunt Clear may be more than she can handle. Can Clear hold it together to help find Grant's daughter before it is too late?

Available in paperback and e-book formats at your favorite e-book or traditional retailer.

End of Time, Book Three in the Castleton Series by Mike Dunbar

In the distant future, technology has disappeared and few humans remain. This remnant lives a simple, peaceful existence; until an unexpected invader arrives. Yellow in color, shaped like a cross between a knight in armor and a football player--- these beings liquefy all the people they find. The villagers call them Dandelions, because they are yellow in color and just popped up out of nowhere. Charlie Newcomb escapes these monsters and travels back seven generations to find the daring innovative time crew described in her ancestor's diary.

Freshly returned from studying the Battle of Agincourt for a UNH professor Mike Castleton, Patrick Weaver and Nick Pope witnessed the power of the English long bow. With this simple weapon, a handful of English archers had destroyed an army of French knights. The CT9225's crew answers Charlie's desperate plea for help. With their friends Allie Tymoshenko, Jen Canfield and Loren Smith they return with Charlie to lead the few unarmed humans into battle with the Dandelion army, and perhaps witness the end of time.

Available in paperback and e-book formats at your favorite e-book or traditional retailer.

.

The Price of Honor, Book 1 in The Lore of Algoron Series By Gus Gallows

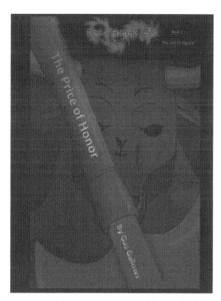

Ganth, the Minotaur Empire, stretching across the continent of Ice Wall within the realm of Algoron, is a place where Honor is the foremost trait among its citizens. Here strength defines law; a law that has left Pah'min in disgrace. His life in Ganth forfeit, his childhood love denied; he is snubbed by all. But there is one House that will accept him. The secret house is despised as an honor-lacking abode of spies. It is from this dark place that Pah'min must begin the long and painful trek to restore his honor. He must begin again in the land of his enemies, and feign loyalty to a king he loathes. There will be many foes on all sides, but his greatest battles are within as the gods themselves try to sway him toward their own mysterious end. Ultimately, he must escape, sacrificing those he holds dear, all to pay the price...The Price of Honor.

The Lost Crew
Book 2 in The Castleton Series
by Mike Dunbar

In book two of the Castleton series Allie, Jen, and their comrade Bashir are sent on a mission to study the roots of Jazz. They follow this music back through time -- from New Orleans, to Paris, and to ancient Carthage. Unbeknownst to the Time Institute the crew are captured and sold into the Roman Empire as slaves.

Mike, Nick, and Patrick are recruited for their first rescue mission. They must retrace the lost crew's steps, discover what happened, and bring their fellow time travelers home. By the time they arrive will their friends be alive or dead? Can they be saved without changing time and setting off Chaos? Do their friends want to be saved? You'll discover once again that time travel messes with your mind and with your heart.

Available in paperback and e-book formats at your favorite e-book or traditional retailer.

Elements of a Broken Mind,
Book 1 in The Clear Angel Chronicles
By Heidi Angell

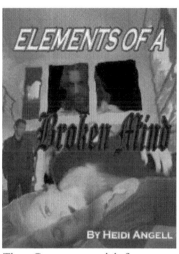

Grant Anderson is a small-town detective whose job was quiet and easy, until three girls end up dead. A serial killer is stalking the young ladies in his town. Without the high tech equipment of big cities at his fingers, Grant must rely on good old-fashioned police work; but with no discernible pattern and no clues to follow, the case seems to be grinding to a halt.

Then Grant gets a visit from a mysterious young woman. Who is Clear Angel? What is her connection to the case? If Grant is to believe her, then he must accept that she has "seen" these things. But Grant is a professional. He cannot believe in psychics! Yet when another girl goes missing, and Grant's search is yielding nothing he is desperate enough to try.

Grant and Clear team up to stop a madman bent on the destruction of the world. As their feelings for one another grow, they try to deny them. But when Clear goes missing, Grant must face his feelings and save her before it is too late.

Available in paperback and e-book formats at your favorite e-book or traditional retailer.

The Hampton Summit
Book 1 in The Castleton Series
by Mike Dunbar

Time travel messes with your mind, and your love life. That's what you'll discover in the Castleton Series, an eight-book romantic/adventure saga for smart, curious readers. The series leads you back to the dawn of humanity, into the distant future, and ends up where it began - messing with your mind all the way.

The Castleton Series is the story of young teens Mike Castleton and Allie Tymoshenko. The pair fall in love, but they are star-crossed, having been born seven generations apart. When Allie meets the boy from the past, she recognizes him as the young Captain Mike Castleton of the band the Sirens. When older, Mike will set off a revolution in music known as Chamber Rock. Allie can never tell Mike about his future, and the mystery surrounding Captain Mike; at the peak of his career, he disappears. In this series you will follow the lovers as they age and mature, and search for happiness. The series will mess with your mind as the couple experiences amazing and dangerous adventures in time.

In this first book The Hampton Summit, Allie and Mike meet when Mike and his friends are recruited by time travelers to prevent a murder in their hometown. A team of renegades from the Time Institute intends to kill a wheelchair-bound scientist before he can share a discovery that creates the peaceful future Allie knows.

The assassins' goal is to rearrange the past so they can dominate the chaotic world they create. Traveling forward in time to be trained at the Institute, the boys are befriended by fellow cadets, Allie, and her roommate, Jen. Using only their wits, the group of innovative and resourceful teens risks their own lives as they take on the team of killers. In the process, Mike and Allie kindle a romance that can never be.

Available in paperback and e-book formats at your favorite e-book or traditional retailer.

The Hunters by Heidi Angell

What would you do if you found your town had been infested with vampires? For Chris and his brother Lucas, the answer was simple enough: you fight back.

Gathering a small band of other people in their town who have been affected by the vampires, they begin a resistance. But after a year of fighting, they have only managed to kill a handful, while the vampire leader has turned five times that many.

Then two enigmatic strangers appear, changing the groups lives even further. Fury and Havoc. They call themselves hunters, and want no part in this little band of heroes. Ordering them to lay low, the duo vow to rid their town of vampires. When Fury is injured, Chris aides these strangers, entwining his future with theirs. Now that the vampires know the hunters are here, and that Chris and his friends have helped them, the group is in more danger than ever before. Lucas is torn between protecting his new family from the vampires, and protecting them from these seemingly inhuman beings who say they are there to help. After all, what beings could be so powerful as to scare a vampire?

Available in paperback and e-book formats at your favorite e-book or traditional retailer.

Angels & Warriors: The Awakening
by Dawn Tevy

In the novel, 'Angels & Warriors, The Awakening,' author Dawn Tevy introduces you to characters that are funny, loving, and artfully scheming... Our heroin, Lady Tynae, finds herself in a precarious situation when she is hunted down by those she most trusts. In a single heartbeat her fairly simple life becomes incredibly complicated. Finding herself in a new world full of magic, dragons, and an old friend, Tynae soon discovers nothing in her life was ever as it appeared. The vivid scenes and descriptive dialogue will transport you to another place. This spectacular fantasy world is set in a time and land that has slowly faded into the haziness of legend and lore. Between discovering her new world and falling in love, Tynae must uncover what lies at her very core. She is accomplished with swords, an expert marksman, and she even knows how to bring a full grown man to his knees...but is she the 'Chosen One'?

Available in paperback and e-book formats at your favorite e-book or traditional retailer.

Made in the USA
Lexington, KY
27 March 2014